It's

Complicated

FRIENDS FOREVER 2

ANITA DAVIS

ISBN-10: 1-946721-03-4
ISBN-13: 978-1-946721-03-7

Books may be purchased in quantity by contacting the author Anita Davis.:
Set Apart Publishing
PO Box 39229
Chicago, IL 60659-0229
or by email at authoranitadavis@gmail.com

ACKNOWLEDGMENTS

Thank you God for giving me the imagination I have, the gift to write, and the time to do it.

Thank you to everyone who supports me as an author and gives me invaluable feedback during the stages of writing my books. To you Gabrielle, Latrease, Michelle, Momma, to name a few.

Thank you to everyone who has purchased copies of my other books and left ratings and reviews on amazon, Goodreads, or emailed me your review. Thank you all for your support.

A special thank you so much to my editor, Michelle, for laboring with me through the revisions and phone conversations. I appreciate the fact that you get me, and I look forward to editing so many more of my books with you for years to come. Get ready! LOL

This one is for Lillian. I hope you enjoy this and that it satisfies you after having to wait for it after you highly enjoyed "Catch Me If You Can".

Painful as it may be, a significant, emotional event can be the catalyst for choosing a direction that serves us—and those around us—more effectively. Look for the learning.

~Louisa May Alcott

1

Melanie left her new journal open sprawled across her bed.

Dear Diary,

Wow. I haven't did this in so long, I mean wrote my thoughts out. I used to love to write daily, along with drawing, but over the years my passion for art dominated my time along with caring for my mother when she had her episodes, but writing in my diary (or should I call it a journal at my age? Lol) now is so needed after all I've been through this past year. Well, let me recap my best friend Karen's life before I get to the details of mine. She was pursued by and fell in love with NBA basketball superstar Kyle Irving. Karen was really starting to let her guard down with him until all of his baby mommas came out of hiding. Three to be exact, but only one child, Gabrielle, ended up being his. She's an adorable little thing. Karen didn't want to be with a pro athlete in the first place because she felt their

1

reputations of being dogs when it comes to women would cause her more pain than pleasure. So, finding out about the baby mommas—especially the two, Porsha and Unique, who turned out not to be baby mommas after all—sent Karen right into the arms of her conniving coworker Dennis Michaels. Ugh! I didn't like him from the beginning and I voiced my opinion about him to Karen because I love her and want the best for her, but since she's grown and she's my best friend, I couldn't do anything but support her right up to her wedding with Dennis. THANK GOD that Kyle crashed it with evidence that Dennis' lying, trifling tail paid off the two pregnant women to claim that Kyle fathered their children and create drama so that he could steal Karen from Kyle. Of course when the truth came out Karen left Dennis' sorry @$$ at the altar. Now Kyle and Karen are back on track. Well, if you think that was something, what happened to me would probably floor you if you were a human and not just the paper I'm writing on. I met Kyle's agent/best friend, Andrew, when they popped up while Karen and I were vacationing in St. Lucia. I know this is cliché but it was love at first sight for us. Like we knew each other our whole lives. Really, it's sickening how close we are to one another versus how we've spent the past months together, but I'll get to that in a second. My mother, Marie Daniels, has always had these weird spells that I've had to tend to her for. She goes into these frantic fits where I have to literally hold her and rock her to calm her down. She's not psychotic or anything, the doctors confirmed that, so I just always figured that it was something from her past that was tormenting her. Come to find out it was a big thing. Andrew and I had gotten real close—I mean real close—but whenever we almost went there, my mom would call and I would have to help her through a spell. He wanted to marry me and I wanted to marry him in time, but with him nagging me about meeting my mom before we got any closer, I knew he and I might not work out because he was big on family. I wasn't ready for him to meet her just yet, because the last time I introduced my mom to a boyfriend of mine she went bananas. She always cautioned me about men and to be careful with them, so I did just that up until Andrew. Remember I told you about Karen and Dennis almost getting married? Well, Andrew showed up at the wedding knowing that my mother would be there. He really wanted to meet her and boy when they met I got the shock of my life. Andrew loved my eyes. He said they always reminded him of someone, from where he couldn't remember, but they held something special for him. Well, I have eyes just like my mother. I was ABSOLUTELY SHOCKED to find out that day as my mother stared into Andrew's eyes and he into hers, she recognized him as the son that she gave away when he was like three or four years old. Ugh!!! I kissed my brother for months! I was in love with my brother! I almost made love to my brother! I threw up at Karen's almost wedding when I found out about it, and now I have to work hard to suppress the urge to throw up whenever I think about it. How will I get over this? And it's not *like I can just forget about it, Andrew's been hounding me trying to hang out with me so we can bond like sister and brother, but I've been ignoring him and my mom until today. I finally agreed to meet with them. Matter of fact, that's my mom calling me on my phone now. She's probably trying to make sure that I'll still meet them at the restaurant. Ugh! I guess I have to deal with my new reality now— getting to know Andrew as my brother when just a month ago he was my boyfriend. I can't hold it in any longer, I have to throw up....*

2

Melanie sat at the table gripping her temples trying to will them from throbbing against her rich, deep, sun-kissed skin. She still couldn't believe the nightmare that she had recently lived and that her life had come to this point—she was about to have lunch with her mother and Andrew, a man she was romantically involved with mere months ago. She shuddered thinking about their many make-out sessions and how close they came to having sex several times.

Her face scrunched up as if she was eating a sour patch kid and she shook her head realizing how disgusting it would've been had they had sex.

She saw Andrew helping her mother get out of the car and quickly realized it was a mistake for her to be there. She still wasn't ready to speak to either of them, but at the same time, she had so many questions that only her mother could answer. She rolled her eyes looking at how chum Andrew and her mother, Marie, were. They walked arm in arm into the restaurant.

Melanie sat up straight in her seat and stared down at the turtleneck she wore. She shook her head again realizing the finicky weather of the autumn Chicago day wasn't what had her wearing the turtleneck. She remembered how only months ago she savored catching Andrew sneaking peeks of her cleavage if she wore a low plunging neckline shirt; but that day she wore the black, shapeless, oversized sweater hoping that it would bottle up all of her that Andrew ever thought was sexy. After all, he was her brother. She wondered how he saw her now, given their newfound relationship to one another.

Her weird thoughts were interrupted by the sweet sound of her mother's voice.

"Melanie, baby, I'm so glad to see you. You look frail though." Marie stretched her arms wide waiting for Melanie to occupy the space between them.

Melanie stood up begrudgingly at first and looked at her mother. She missed her. She had never gone this long without seeing and talking to her mother. She looked different. She seemed more vibrant. The once vacant stare she always seemed to harbor was now replaced with an unspeakable merriment.

Melanie stepped into her mother's arms and rested her chin on Marie's shoulder. She cried as Marie's warm hug engulfed her. For a moment, the past few months hadn't occurred and Melanie relished in her mother's presence but Andrew clearing his throat brought her back into that space and time, the reason why she was there.

Melanie wiped any trace of tears from her eyes as she pulled back from her mother.

Marie cupped Melanie's now slender face and placed a long, gentle kiss on her forehead. "Baby, please don't ever stay away from me this long. It's been over three months. Not talking to you hurts."

Melanie wiped the tears from Marie's face. "I know, Mom, but I just needed some time to clear my head and try to make sense of what happened, but I couldn't because I need answers from you. That's why I'm here."

"Hi, Melanie." Andrew cleared his throat. He stood behind the chair for Marie waiting to tuck her in at the table.

Marie smiled.

Melanie swallowed the bile that formed in her mouth. She wasn't ready to deal with him but her mother insisted that he be there.

Deep down inside, Melanie knew none of it was his fault, but she still wasn't ready to face him.

"Hey." She said barely audible with her back still facing him.

Marie sat and patted Andrew's hand thanking him for seating her.

Andrew. Melanie thought to herself how his name used to drip like honey from her lips and how she used to love gazing into his eyes, but now she was across from him not saying his name when she spoke and refusing to make eye contact with him. She folded her arms across her chest and stared out the window of the restaurant at nothing at all.

"Melanie. Melanie," Marie called out.

"Ma'am." Melanie was careful to look at her mother and not at Andrew sitting close to Marie.

"Come on, Melanie. We have to talk at some point. You are my sister," Andrew said.

Melanie turned to him with a venomous stare. "And you don't find that repulsive? That I'm your sister? But what, four-five months ago, I was half-naked in my bedroom ready to make love to you." Melanie looked around her to make sure that no one had heard her incestuous rant.

"Melanie, don't you think I feel some kind of way about this?" Andrew paused. He took deep breaths to calm himself down. He lowered his voice before he said, "I wanted to marry you, so yes, how we turned out weirds me out, but you of all people know how much I wanted to meet my birth mother, so as crazy as it sounds, I'm glad you and I met because it caused me to reconnect with her." He looked to Marie. He grabbed her hand and squeezed it.

"I thought I could, but I can't take this. I have to get out of here." Melanie stood and grabbed her jacket hanging on the back of her chair.

"Sit down now."

Melanie heard the stern tone in her mother's voice and painstakingly took her seat. She refused to look at either of them.

"You listen to me, young lady. I'm sorry that I didn't tell you about Andrew, I just couldn't." Marie choked on the tears in her throat. She got up and sat in the empty seat next to Melanie. She grabbed Melanie's hand and squeezed it tightly. She then grabbed Melanie's chin forcing her to look her in the eyes. She sighed before speaking again. "I did what made sense to me at that time. You saw how tormented I was. I'm not that way anymore and I have you and him to thank for that." She looked over at Andrew and smiled.

Melanie's face remained stoic. "Okay, so you're here to give me some answers to my questions. Who is Andrew's father? Did you ever report the rape?" Melanie's face softened hoping her last question wasn't too insensitive.

Marie sat silent staring at the wood grains in the table flowing freely from one pattern into another. She wished the revelation of her rape and the aftermath of it would flow as effortless into understanding and forgiveness with her children as the shifting wood grain patterns. But with Melanie putting up resistance to the shift, she wished she were anywhere else but there at that moment.

"Mom, you know me. I love you. I could've handled knowing what happened to you and the fact that I have a brother." Melanie still hated admitting that she had a brother, especially considering he was Andrew.

Andrew chimed in. "I just wish I didn't have to pay for what he did to you. Me growing up without you and you in my life." He looked at Marie and then at Melanie.

Melanie turned away from him.

He shook his head in frustration.

"Melanie, I wanted us all to come together today to move forward, not dwell in the past. Please don't bring up asking me how Drew came to be. I'm still

not ready to talk about that. I don't think I ever will
be."

3

Kyle pulled her in closer to him burying his chin into her scalp. He wanted to inhale more of the warm scent her short and cropped hair held. "K?"

She stirred. "What?"

"I'm so glad that you're here with me instead of being married to Dennis right now."

Her eyes were bright and glossy. "Kyle, you keep saying that."

"I can't help it. That's exactly how I feel."

"Well, he and I weren't really meant to be so that's why it didn't work out."

"I knew that all along, but it seemed like you didn't know that for a while."

"I thought I loved him." Karen pouted her thin mouth.

"You could never really love that creep."

"Whatever." Karen smiled and jabbed Kyle in his side. "You didn't know that he was a creep at first."

"Yes, I did. I knew from day one that he was no good for you."

Karen rolled over on her side and propped herself on her elbow giving her the perfect view of Kyle's chiseled abs as he laid in the bed next to her. She got lost in his dark brown eyes. She refocused her thoughts back to their discussion at hand. "Why didn't you tell me that he was a creep?"

Kyle cleared his throat. "What do you mean, I didn't tell you? I tried to when you and I were together but you dumped me and stopped talking to me." Kyle lowered his head feigning offense to Karen's past actions towards him.

Karen leaned forward as she gathered herself to kiss him on his soft lips. He grabbed her and tried to deepen the kiss, but she pushed him back. He acquiesced and continued speaking. "Remember *you* wouldn't even give me the time of day to really tell you anything about him."

"Oh yeah." Karen rested her dark, brown fingertip on her chin pretending to remember what Kyle was referencing.

He smirked at her. "Yeah, really. I didn't know how much of a creep he was until my lawyer came back with the information about Porsha and Unique."

Karen rolled her slanted eyes. "Why'd you have to mention those two?"

"Sorry, I didn't mean to," Kyle said.

"Well, don't do it again."

"Right. Thank God I don't have to deal with them ever again. I couldn't imagine having to deal with those two bearing my children."

"Well, that's what happens when you sleep with any and everybody." Karen sucked her teeth in annoyance of Kyle's past.

He grabbed her and pulled her close to him and kissed the top of her head. "I know, babe, but that's my past. You're the only one I plan on sleeping with." He squeezed her butt as his eyebrows lifted up and down rapidly suggesting what he wanted from her.

She smacked his hands from her backside. "Yeah, and it won't happen anytime soon. Since we haven't done it yet, we might as well wait 'til marriage."

"What you talking 'bout, Willis?" Kyle recited the famous one liner from the hit sitcom *Different Strokes*. His eyebrows wrinkled as he stared at Karen. "Wait 'til marriage? You mean no nookie 'til we're married?" Kyle frowned.

"Yes, no nookie." Karen smiled. "We might as well wait 'til after we're married. Besides, I think that if we wait, it will strengthen our relationship. It will give us the chance to really get to know each other outside of having sex."

Kyle sighed as he rubbed his head. "Yeah, I understand that that's a way a couple can really get to know each other, but come on, Karen. We've known each other long enough to know that we love each other, and since we are getting married, I think it'll be okay if I sampled the milk before I buy the cow. Trust me, I love the cow." Kyle rolled over onto Karen and began to plant wet, soft kisses on her neck causing her to squirm in desire under him.

"Kyle. Kyle. Stop. I'm being serious here." She gave him a strong enough shove that lifted him off her. He sighed and fell back onto his back. She sat up Indian style in the bed and stared at him. "And who are you calling a cow?"

Kyle smiled and shook his head at the confrontational stance Karen held with her hands on her hips. "I'm not saying you look like a cow. I was using the analogy to say that why don't you just let me sample the goods before I buy what's in the store." Kyle winked at her.

Karen snatched the pillow from behind his head and raised it above her head gathering enough strength to get a good swing on him with it, but Kyle began tickling her sides causing her to laugh hysterically and drop the pillow.

"I'm kidding with you. Come here." He caught her by her waist before she tried to jump out of the bed to escape him tickling her. He pulled her into his arms and held her tightly. She finally rested in his arms and he interlaced his hand with hers and brushed her hair out of her face. "So now that Unique, Porsche, and Dennis are out of the way, we can continue building our relationship." He kissed the top of her head again as he had become so fond of doing.

"Well, we still have some other things that are in the way."

"Like what?" Kyle looked down at her chest which was no longer heaving up and down. It looked to him as if she was holding her breath. He lifted up off the pillow some to get a better look at her face. "Like what?"

"Mercedes and Gabrielle," Karen uttered.

Kyle sat up straight forcing Karen to sit up as well.

Karen knew that Kyle's eyebrows drawing closer together meant he was waiting to see if she would further explain her statement. She cleared her throat and continued to speak. "I'm not saying that they are in the way like in a bad way, but we have to keep in mind it will never only be you and I."

Kyle's jaws tightened. Karen knew she needed to say more to better explain her feelings about his daughter. She reached out and grabbed his hands into hers. She looked lovingly into his eyes. "Of course I love Gabby because she's yours, and I look forward to getting to know her more, but because she has a mother that's not me, we will always have to take her mother's, Mercedes, feelings and thoughts into consideration when we're doing things and making decisions. Nothing we ever do will just be about you and me."

Kyle stared at Karen for a minute taking in her thin mouth but plump lips before he looked into her eyes. Eyes that told him she loved him. He pulled her hand up to his face allowing the back of it to caress his cheek before he said, "I know this is not the life that you planned for yourself, being with a man who has a kid that's not yours, but as you have seen, Mercedes is cool. She and I have nothing going on that you ever need to worry about. She simply a fling. We never had feelings for one another so you don't have to worry about any old feelings resurfacing." He searched Karen's eyes gauging if she believed him.

After moments of staring into his deep brown eyes, a smile crept across her face and said. "Yeah, I could tell that there isn't anything between you and her, or at least I hope it's not." Karen pursed her lips.

Kyle smiled and commenced to tickling Karen again to lighten up the mood. She giggled as he pulled her closer to him.

She nestled in his arms again taking in the lingering sporty scent of his cologne.

He held on tightly to her as he said, "I know that you would've loved for it just to be you and me, but hey, and least you'll have one less birth to go through as you sacrifice your body to give me the rest of my starting lineup. You'll only have to have four babies instead of five." A wide grin crept across his face and he tried to kiss her but she pulled back from him as her eyes widened.

"Four kids? Who do you think is going to have four of your rock head kids?" She rubbed his smooth, bald head.

"You."

"You are out of your mind, Mr. Irving. But just to humor me some more, who's going to raise those four kids of ours?"

"We will. You," he pecked her lips with his, "and I will." He kissed her again.

His inviting kisses temporarily suspended her thought process. She held onto his face allowing her tongue to explore his mouth before she pulled back from him to gather more information. "No, seriously, who's going to carry each of those four kids of yours for ten months each?" Karen continued speaking, ignoring Kyle's rapidly blinking eyes. "We're in our early thirties now, but by the time we get married and enjoy one another, we may be into our mid and late thirties. Who's having four kids knocking on forty?" Karen scratched her temple waiting for Kyle to respond.

"Ten months? I thought women were only pregnant for nine months." Kyle's thick eyebrows furrowed.

"Nope. See how you're making plans for a woman's body and you don't even know how long she'll have to bare each of your seeds."

"Look woman, I swear if I could I would but since I can't, you're the lucky winner."

"Whatever. Look, Kyle, I love you and I do want to have kids with you after we're married, but I can't afford to have four kids. Four pregnancies will put me out of commission for far too long. You know the lifespan of a news reporter, let alone a sports broadcaster, is short. I have to ride my wave for as long as I can."

Kyle could only respect her career ambitions since he planned to play basketball for as long as he physically could. "So if you don't want four kids, then how many are you willing to give me?" Kyle raised one eyebrow staring at Karen as he awaited her response.

"Mmm, I say one and a possible. But if we're really smart, we could shoot for twins the first time around and then we wouldn't even have to try after that." Karen smiled.

"Yeah, you say that now woman, but when I get done with you, you will be begging me to give you more kids." Kyle flashed her a winning smile. He stretched his long, muscular limbs.

She stared at his smooth, caramel skin. "Whatever." Karen rolled her slanted eyes.

"So how is Melanie doing?"

Karen got up from the bed and searched the floor for her slippers. She slid her feet into the comfy pockets of air.. "How do you think she's doing?"

Kyle rubbed his chin and you could hear the rustling of his goatee. He needed to shave. "I can't imagine how she feels to have been in love with her brother."

"You tell me how Andrew feels? He's your best friend." Karen allowed Kyle to pull her in between his legs as they now dangled off the edge of the bed.

"He's pretty okay with it."

"Hunh?" Karen asked in amazement.

"Yeah, he thinks his mind was telling him to get to know her to uncover the truth, not uncover her nakedness, but of course we know what head led him these past months."

Karen stiffened in Kyle's arms. "So what are you saying, he never loved Melanie? He was just trying to have sex with her?"

"No. I know Melanie is your best friend. Y'all are like sisters and have been since you all were in high school. You're ready to come to her defense, but I didn't do anything wrong to her, so don't jump down

18

my throat." Kyle rubbed Karen's shoulders trying to knead the knots that had quickly formed in them. "And you know as well as I do that he really did love her, it wasn't just lust. In hindsight, he believes that maybe they really did confuse their attraction for one another as romantic when it really was just designed for them to know one another to unveil their truth. You know he's always wanted to know his blood family and she ultimately was the key to unlock his past and lead him to his mother." Kyle sighed. "He's hoping that they can move past it and build a brother-sister relationship because he wants to be around his mother as much as possible and Melanie keeping her distance from him is kind of putting a strain on the three of them coming together."

Karen rolled her eyes at Kyle. "Duh. What if the woman you were in love with for months turned out to be your sister? Would you be so willing and eager to see her as your sister? Why should she have to forget her recent past so quick? That's a lot for a woman."

Kyle shook his head. "Yeah, you all are emotional creatures."

Karen pushed Kyle really hard in the chest this time.

"Hey." Kyle's body stiffened as his eyes widened. He smiled with a knowing look. "Why'd you do that?"

"Because, you called us emotional creatures."

"I'm sorry, baby. You're a beautiful, emotional creature."

"Yeah, whatever."

"Hold on, that's my phone." Kyle grabbed his phone from the nightstand.

Karen saw Mercedes name flashed brightly across the screen. She rolled her eyes.

"Hello?" After a short pause, he said, "Okay. I'll be right there in a minute." He hung up the phone and felt Karen tense up in his arms again. "I'm sorry, baby, I have to go. Something's come up with Gabby."

"We were supposed to go to breakfast this morning."

"I know. We'll have to reschedule." He studied her face. "I love you, Karen." He tried to kiss her but she turned her head away pouting. "Don't be like that." He drew her in to him. "I said we'll reschedule." He buried his face in the nape of her neck and smothered her with kisses.

She worked hard to pull back from him. "So is this what I have to look forward to every time Mercedes calls, you go running?"

4

Karen let herself into Melanie's condo. "Melanie? Mel?" She turned her head from left to right searching for Melanie as she headed to the master bedroom where she normally found Melanie in the bathroom or closet. "Mel, where are you?"

She scrunched her nose and held her breath intermittently trying to obscure her nostrils of the putrid odor coming from somewhere in the condo. She walked back out the bedroom and searched the other rooms around the house and even the balcony, which gave her a breath of fresh air and relief of the stinging odor in the condo. She knew for sure that Melanie wasn't at home.

She walked back to the kitchen and took out her cell phone, pressed two on her keypad and Melanie's number popped up on the screen. She pressed the call button.

Melanie answered after a few rings. "Hello."

"Where are you? Because you certainly aren't home." Karen wrote "clean me" in the dust that had collected on the kitchen countertop. She sneezed.

"How do you know that? Wait, you're in my condo, aren't you?" Melanie shook her head.

"You know I am, but why aren't you?" Karen scrunched her face yet again getting nauseous from the horrific odor that seemed to be emanating from the refrigerator.

"I'm at my gallery."

"You're having a showing tonight and you didn't invite me?" Karen pouted, pretending her feelings were really hurt.

"No. Quit your whining." Melanie laughed a little. "The gallery is closed. I'm in my studio in the back trying to paint. And why are you in my place? I gave you a spare key in case I ever got locked out or something that required immediate attention and I couldn't get there in time," Melanie said.

"Or, for the times you've needed me to grab something you left here and bring it down to the gallery. Also the reason why you gave me a key to your gallery." Karen rolled her eyes playfully knowing Melanie couldn't see the gesture.

"Whatever, don't act like I'm so forgetful of things. We both have keys to each other's places in the event of emergencies." Melanie adjusted herself on her stool.

"Yeah, emergencies." Karen cackled as her head titled back. "I guess we have emergencies daily. We always let ourselves into each other's places."

Melanie smiled. "Right."

"Besides, I came over here looking for you. I've missed you." Karen continued holding her breath to keep from inhaling the horrible smell circulating in Melanie's place.

"I can't tell. You've been spending all your time with Kyle when you're not taping a show. Lately, I only see you once in a while when we run together. You're *my* best friend." Melanie pouted.

"Oh whatever. We can change that now. We can have a girls' day. I'll order some pizza. I already have the ice cream, and we can let the TV watch us while we catch up."

"Nah, I'm just gonna stay here and paint."

"Forget what I said we should do, because clearly from this smell in your house, we need to be in here cleaning up. It really stinks in here, Mel." Karen walked towards the front door.

"Yeah, I've been in such a funk that I haven't even cleaned my house...I'll catch up with you another day." Melanie ended the call.

Karen locked Melanie's door and rushed across the hall to her condo to grab her purse.

"Whatever. If you don't come to me, I'll come to you."

***

Karen stood at the front door of Melanie's art gallery. She saw no signs of Melanie. Believing Melanie was still in her studio in the back of the gallery, she used her key to let herself in.

Karen slowly walked through the gallery taking in many of the newer pieces that Melanie had acquired. She frowned, not seeing any hanging that reflected Melanie's fingerprint.

She walked into Melanie's studio to see her idly sitting on a stool staring at an almost blank canvas in front of her. She became worried for her friend. Normally Melanie's flow with painting was effortless and she always managed to create some of the most eye catching pieces ever.

"Mel? Sweetie, I'm here." Melanie seemed a little bit more chipper on the phone than the Melanie she was now looking at. She walked closer to her, not sure if she had taken on the catatonic like behavior her mother had months ago; before they all found out who Andrew really was.

Melanie came out of her daze to see Karen in the room. "I should've known you would come down here. You act like we haven't seen each other in forever, but I just saw you when we ran together the other day."

"Yeah, but we don't talk much during our runs." Karen pouted. "You seem to love it now more than I do."

"I always loved it. I just liked to give you a hard time pretending not to." Melanie stuck her tongue out. "But yeah, running seems to be the only time thoughts of almost having sex with my brother stay at bay." Melanie stuck her finger in her mouth pretending to make herself gag.

Karen smiled. "Yeah, I hear ya." She slowly walked over to a wall full of Melanie's paintings. She stared at them in awe for a while before she said, "I don't get you."

"What?" Melanie turned her attention to where she heard the sound of Karen's voice.

"You are an amazing artist and yet you barely put your work on display anymore. I'm certain you have more pieces than these hanging. You could fill up wall after wall in the gallery out there. Your paintings would sell like hotcakes as they used to if you would only put them out there." Karen went closer to one and touched it trying to gauge what type of materials Melanie may have used to bring the painting to life the way it seemed to pop off the canvas.

It was one of Melanie's favorites and latest that Karen ogled.

Karen turned towards Melanie. "Seriously, Melanie, if you don't put them up in your studio, I'm going to take some of them and sell them on eBay, and I won't give you any of the money I make from them." Karen pursed her lips trying to hold her laughter in.

Melanie shook her head laughing. "Whatever. I'm not much in a sharing mood with my pieces right now. Maybe if I die before you, you can sell them then."

"Oh hush talking about death. You and I both will live long, healthy, and prosperous lives."

"That's easy for you to say. You have everything that you've ever wanted right now, the career you've always wanted, and the man of your dreams."

"Well, yes, my career is where I want it to be for now, but that man of mine, that didn't start off as my dream romance, more like a nightmare."

They both chortled.

"Oh yeah, you've had an interesting year, too. Met Kyle, got close to him, but then got scared of being with him and ran right into the arms of that creep Dennis." Melanie's lips formed into a snarl recounting the past year. "I can't believe you almost married that creep, who, might I add, basically manipulated you into dating him. All to keep you away from Kyle. I never did like him. But I swear you weren't dealt the blow I was dealt." Melanie slumped her shoulders.

"We won't go tit for tat with who had the worst past year. Let's just work on making better futures."

"You sound like my mother." Melanie stood up from her stool. She walked over to her shelf of paints and grabbed more colors.

Karen put her purse down on a shelf near the paints and pulled a stool close to Melanie's.

Melanie sat back down.

"Speaking of your mother, how did it go with her and Andrew when you finally met with them? How did it feel being around him?"

They both visibly shuddered.

"I was happy to see my mother. I missed not seeing her these past months I've avoided her. You know how much of a rock I've had to be for her over the years."

"Yeah," Karen agreed.

"She seemed so much happier yesterday, more lively, despite not willing to admit who Andrew's father is and really tell us the story behind that." Melanie slashed another long red stroke across her canvas. It ran parallel with the one she had drawn since Karen had been there.

"Wow. Yeah, I know you and Andrew want answers from her, but keep in mind having been raped must still be something difficult for her to deal with. Probably always will be."

"Yeah, I thought about that when I was talking to her. I really do sympathize with her on that. It's just that the aftermath of it is what's affecting me now. I mean come on, I'm a perfect episode of the *Maury* show. I can see it now, Maury sitting on stage with me next to him. *Ladies and gentleman. Here we have Melanie Daniels, a woman who was in love with her brother unbeknownst to her.* The crowd will go wild with their 'ooohs' and 'aahhs' and I'd be the most sympathy given woman slash laughing stock of the world."

Karen sat staring incredulously at Melanie. "Wow, Mel. Now I know that I can be dramatic at times, but I think you just won an award for that tale you just spun." Karen shook her head.

Melanie gave her a half smile.

"So if she's not willing to tell you all who his father is, will you be able to move on past this? Are you going to try and build a relationship with Andrew, your brother?"

They both shuddered and then there heads fell back and their mouths opened wide as their laughter filled the room at the automaticity of their action.

"You know we're going to have to stop doing that at some point." Karen softly chuckled.

"I know, but the mere mention of Andrew being my brother automatically evokes that response from my body."

They shuddered again and then almost fell off their stools from laughing so hard.

The sun had set outside and the artificial lighting in the studio promoted a more docile atmosphere for their conversation.

Melanie held her dry paintbrush at her side ready to be transparent with her best friend. She turned to face Karen. "I know it's not Andrew's fault that we fell in love only to find out that we're brother and sister. Yes I know that the *right* thing to do is to quickly move past what we had and work to build a brother-sister friendship. Maybe I'll get there one day; but I don't know when that day will be."

"Yeah, I hear ya. Soooo, are you jumping back on the saddle soon or what?"

Melanie bucked her neck at Karen. "Seriously? Getting with a man is the least of my concerns at this point in my life."

Karen displayed a mischievous wide grin. "It may be what you need to get you out of your funk and help you move on."

"Just because that worked with you and Kyle does not mean that'll work for me."

"I beg your pardon?" Karen laid a flat palm over her chest and her eyes widened as if she was appalled.

"Seriously, you got over Dennis with Kyle." Melanie sang Kyle's name.

"Oh whatever." Karen waved her hand dismissively at Melanie. "According to you, I was never really in love with Dennis. I said yes to his proposal as a means of avoiding Kyle, but you see where that landed me."

"Yeah, right in Kyle's arms."

"So, it's possible that that can work for you as well."

"I doubt it. I'm thinking like when I do get back into dating, it would probably be safe if it's with a white guy."

Karen cocked her head and bucked her eyes at Melanie. "Are you serious?"

"Yes. Why are you looking at me like that?"

"You, Afrocentric Melanie." She reached out and patted Melanie's curly, fluffy, coif. "Would you seriously date outside of your race? And a white guy at that?"

"Why is that so unbelievable?" Melanie picked up her brush, dipped it into more red paint, and began to stroke the canvas.

"Because you're so pro black." Karen pumped her fist in the air as if she were posing for a "black pride" picture.

"Dating outside of my race wouldn't change me being pro black."

"Seriously, Mel. You've never let on before that you would date someone other than a black man, so this is kind of shocking to me."

Melanie with raised eyebrows turned to face Karen. "So if I did, would you judge me? Would you stop being my friend?"

"Of course not." Karen jumped off her stool and threw her arms around Melanie's neck squeezing it tightly.

"Back off. You're smothering me." Melanie playfully pushed Karen away from her.

"Seriously though, Karen, I have no desire to date anytime soon. I can't say that I would even be comfortable dating a white guy, even though it's 2015. But hey, that's neither here nor there because dating altogether is the furthest thing from my mind. Enough about me, what about you and Kyle?" Melanie tilted her head to the side. "Will I be buying another maid of honor dress soon?" She dipped her brush in the green paint and began to make sense of the red parallel strokes already on the canvas.

Karen smiled. "I'm not sure. I'm just enjoying the space we're in right now." Karen twitched her face.

"You're lying. What's wrong with you two already?"

"How'd you know?" Karen's eyebrows knitted together as she looked at Melanie.

"From that twitch in your face."

"Okay, okay, okay. Possible baby momma drama, but I didn't come here to talk about me. I'm checking up on you."

Melanie stared down Karen hoping it would make her fess up.

"Mel, I promise I'm okay. Kyle and I will be fine." She kept her face void of any tell-tale signs this time. "I'm here for you. How are you?"

"I'm good, or I'm certain I will be in time." Melanie shrugged her shoulders and relaxed into composing the art in front of her.

Karen stared at Melanie's blending technique for a while and the shape she was forming with the colors.

"Look, honey, I know that painting has always been your way of zoning out and dealing with things, but your place really does stink and you have gotten smaller." Karen scanned Melanie from head to toe. "And not because you intentionally tried to lose weight, but because you haven't been taking care of yourself properly."

Melanie looked down at herself. "I look that bad? My mom said something like that about me, too."

"I mean of course you're still gorgeous, but you do kind of look like you've gone on a hunger strike. And that smell in your house, pee-eww!" Karen scrunched up her nose and waved her hand in front of it. "You've got to take care of its source ASAP before that smell makes its way over to my place."

"Whatever." Melanie smiled as she continued with her painting.

"How about this? How about I give you another hour here to finish this creation I might wanna buy from you and then I help you clean up your apartment?"

"An hour? So now you're giving me a curfew?" Melanie turned to stare at Karen who was picking up her purse from the nearby shelf.

Karen looked Melanie directly into her eyes. "Yes. I would drag you out of here now, but I can tell you need a moment with this piece before you head home. But trust and believe I'll be back to drag you out of here if need be." Karen tightened her lips with the intent to appear stern in front of Melanie.

"Okay, Mom," Melanie teased.

"Yeah, whatever. An hour, Mel," Karen said over her shoulder as she headed into the gallery. "I'll have the pizza and ice cream ready, too," she yelled, making sure Melanie would hear her.

Melanie heard the chime at the front door letting her know Karen had walked through it.

She looked down at her wrists. They were thinner than what they normally were. "Do I really look that bad?" She shrugged her shoulders and finally allowed herself to get lost in her painting.

5

Marie pulled the pie out of the oven and placed it on the stove. She laughed at herself when she looked back at the countertop to see the Marie Callender's box the pie was once in. She was never much of a cook, especially with her ongoing frantic episodes over the years, but she wanted to have something for Andrew to munch on when he came over. She had no choice but to buy a pie.

She had to admit to herself that her life was so much better now that she was reconnecting with Andrew. She still couldn't shake the sadness in her heart of how his presence seemed to keep Melanie distant from her. She loved both of her kids and wished that sooner than later they could all become one happy family.

Her doorbell rang.

As she had been doing lately, she thanked God that Andrew and Melanie hadn't slept together. She knew that really would've killed any chance of her kids building a sibling relationship. She opened the door and smiled. "Hi, Drew." She spread her arms wide and he walked into them.

"Hi, Mom." He hugged her tightly treasuring the fact that she was now back in his life.

Marie smiled wide as she continued to hold on to Andrew. She wanted each hug she gave him to say how much she really did love him and to possibly make up for all the hugs she missed giving him when he was growing up. She loved him calling her 'Mom'. It felt so genuine to her.

They finally let go of one another and she stepped aside to let him in the house.

"It smells good in here." Andrew walked over to the mantle on the fireplace to look at pictures of Marie with Melanie when they were younger.

Marie started towards the kitchen. "Yes, I bought an apple pie and heated it up. I have ice cream, too, if you want some."

Andrew had only been to Marie's house three times up to that point and never before had he seen the picture he was now looking at of him and her. He stared at it assuming he was maybe one years old as she held him on her lap. His face lit up with giddiness, while Marie bore a straight face with a blank stare.

The picture said so much to him.

Ever since he found out why she gave him up, he tried to empathize with her for having gone through a horrific ordeal such as rape, but he really wished that Marie hadn't despised him because of who his daddy was. He had long settled with himself before he ever met her that he wouldn't hold back on loving his birth mom if he ever met her no matter the reason that she gave him up.

Marie stood in the kitchen doorway staring at Andrew as he looked at one of the only photos she had of her and him as a little boy. Out of the five she had with him, it was the one where she had the most upbeat facial expression. She wouldn't have dared put one of the other four up of them. Anyone would clearly see the disdain she had for him in her eyes and body language. So yes, the one he looked at of her with the blank stare was the most jovial looking picture she had with him.

She said softly, "Andrew, let's go in the kitchen."

He continued to stare at the picture. "Okay." He finally pulled himself away from the daunting image of him and Marie and followed the scent of the pie to the kitchen. By the time he made it there, Marie already had his pie a la mode on the table.

He sat down, as directed, in front of his plate. "Thanks." He looked up smiling at her and was glad that he didn't see the same look in her eyes as was on the picture on the mantle.

She sat across from him. "So how have you been? I know I just saw you the other day, but with the way Melanie was, we didn't have the time and opportunity to talk as I would've liked for us to."

Andrew finished chewing before he said, "Yeah, I've definitely wanted to spend even more time with you, but I've been really busy with my clients."

"I understand." Marie smiled.

"Thanks. But yeah, I can understand Melanie though. We were in love months ago. I had told her I wanted to marry her."

Marie's eyes widened.

"I know, right?" Andrew laughed a little, shaking his head. "So with us being the way we were, then to find out we're brother and sister, which meant you had a child she knew nothing about, I can see how that would shift her attitude."

"I know. That's why I haven't pushed her too much. I know she needs some time and space to come to terms with everything. I'm certain she'll come around in time. She really is a sweet girl."

"Yeah, she is," Andrew said.

Marie raised an eyebrow as she stared at him smiling. "Andrew, you aren't still in love with her, are you?"

Andrew held up one finger signaling to Marie to give him a moment. He took time clearing his throat several times to prevent from choking on his food at Marie's question. "No, ma'am! I always had the desire to protect Melanie and be there for her. I promise you," he held his right hand up in the air, "I don't see her that way anymore. That day at the church when you confessed to being my mother, I looked over at her and all I saw was my little sister." Andrew reached for the glass of water near his plate and gulped it down trying to fully clear his throat.

"Okay. I believe you, if you say so." She gave him the side eye.

"I'm serious. I guess because I always wondered about you and whether or not I actually had any biological brothers and sisters, I was mentally ready to accept who she really was to me at that exact moment. I wish I could tell her that so that she and I could move forward, start the healing process, but she won't talk to me."

Marie pushed her plate aside, pulled her chair in closer under the table, and intertwined her hands together under her chin. "You don't have to answer any of my questions if you don't want to, but how was it growing up for you?" Marie bit her lip hoping Andrew wouldn't tell her he had a horrible childhood all because she gave him away.

"It was great." Andrew wiped his mouth with his napkin.

Marie got up from the table, grabbed a pitcher of water, and poured more for him.

"Thanks."

"You're welcome. So how are your parents?" Marie was sad thinking about how someone else was responsible for the outstanding man that Andrew was.

"They are the best. They helped me to understand adoption from day one, but they didn't treat me any different from my brother and sister. In fact, they brag on me saying I'm my dad's favorite."

Marie feigned a smile.

Andrew studied Marie's slumped shoulders, the frown on her face and noted her somber mood. "I'm sure you would've been a great mom to me, too."

She couldn't fake her smile any longer. She let out a deep sigh and let the corners of her mouth droop before she said, "I'm not so sure about that. I was pretty much always depressed after..." Marie's words trailed off thinking about her rape.

Andrew sat silent.

"Enough about that. Tell me more about your family."

"Wanna see some pictures of them?"

"Sure."

Andrew pulled his beeping phone out of his pocket. "The battery is really low, but let's see if you can see a few pics before it completely dies."

"Okay." Marie fiddled with her fingers while waiting for Andrew.

"I'm sorry, but every time I try to open my picture gallery a message pops up saying to plug in phone to charger immediately. It won't let me into the gallery."

"That's okay. I can see them another time. Your last name is Dodson, right?" Marie's eyebrows knitted closer together. He had told her his last name since they had reconnected and it had resonated more and more with her, but she opted to dismiss the idea storming in her head.

"Yes."

"Which is your adoptive parents' last name, right?"

Andrew looked at Marie. Her face mirrored that of the one he stared at earlier on the mantle. "Are you okay?" He reached over and squeezed her hand. "It's like you went somewhere else."

"Uh, um, I'm not sure. Don't worry about it. I'll be fine." Marie wrung her hands together.

"Look, Mom, I know how I came to be was bad for you, but for so long, I've wanted to know my birth parents. I thank God I finally met you. Trust me when I say I'm going to do all I can to help us make up the time lost between us over the years, but I've always wanted to know both of my birth parents. Meeting you let me know that I have Melanie as a sister. I want to know who he is. Learn if I'm anything like him? If I have other brothers and sisters?"

Marie stood up from the table and walked over to the kitchen sink. She washed her hands for no apparent reason. "Trust me, you don't want to meet him."

Andrew got up and cautiously approached Marie.

"Marie, Mom. I want to know who my dad is. I feel I have the right to know."

She dried her hands on a towel near the sink and turned to face him. She wanted to be callous in talking to him, get him to see how serious she was, but when she looked into his deep brown eyes, she softened her tone before she said, "Andrew, I wish it were different, but it's not. I will never utter that man's name again. I won't ever tell you who your real father is and there is nothing, you, Melanie, or anyone else could ever say or do to convince me otherwise."

6

Melanie stood in the first corral of runners for the 10k run.

Her morning runs had become a safe haven for her, and after finding out Andrew's true relation to her, she wanted to amp up the amount of running she did. If she could only feel the way she did all day the way she felt when she ran, her life would be so much better.

The announcer signaled for her group to take off running and so she did. Although she admitted to herself that she had slimmed down even more than she naturally was, her weight loss didn't affect her endurance for her runs.

She wasn't focused on how fast she ran, she just needed to run. Her feet hit the pavement hard. Through her feet, she tried to push out every ounce of the mixed emotions she had been harboring for the past couple of months. She shook her head at herself wishing it were that simple.

All she heard as she ran was the sound of her feet thumping the ground and the melodic sound of her heartbeat pulsing in her ear under her headband.

She tried her best to smile back at those that ran near her as they settled into their strides, but her smile didn't fully manifest until she passed the one mile marker. She knew it would be smooth sailing after that. For the average runner, getting past the first mile was the hardest part of a race, depending on the length of the race. Once their bodies glided into that second mile, it settled into its mission, which was to make it to the end, and strong.

With each mile ran, she smiled more and more relishing in her peaceful thoughts, void of Andrew and her mother. *I have to make sure to sign up for an even longer run next time.*

She didn't bother to tell Karen about the run because she knew that although Karen loved to run, and was especially competitive during races, she was at the studio taping her segment or possibly somewhere smooching with Kyle. She laughed out loud thinking about how those two seemed inseparable lately.

At least one of us is happy and gets the love that we want. Oh enough thinking about them, let me get back in my free zone and finish this run strong. Melanie sped up thinking she might possibly beat her time from the last time she ran that distance.

***

Aaron hated that she sped up when he was almost close enough to her to get her attention. He had seen her about two weekends earlier at a last minute 5k he decided to do. He was taken aback by her. Yes, she was beautiful on the outside with her thin, almond shaped eyes, smooth chocolate skin, and he had to admit he loved the way her fluffy hair framed her face, but there was a meekness about her that day that touched him. On one hand she seemed sad and out of touch with life, but the moment she took off running her spirit seemed to come alive in her stride and it called out to him.

Instead of focusing on his running speed during the race, he trailed her with a nice distance between them imagining what type of woman she might be. Would he really be able to get a woman like her? After all she was black and he was white.

Yeah, he knew it was 2015, decades removed from Jim Crow laws and desegregation, but given the race relations in the country, he wouldn't be surprised if she turned him down, *if* he worked up the courage to approach her.

He didn't work up the nerve to approach her the first time he saw her, but he told himself if he ever saw her again he would. He looked at her and noting the gait of her stride, to him, it almost seemed like she needed that run; time alone with her thoughts. *But the next time I see her, I'm making my move.* His smile couldn't be contained as he settled into a jogging pace.

7

Aaron thought about her a lot since the last time he saw her at the last 10k run. He smiled after looking up from stretching his hamstrings to see that she was standing in his corral warming up for the race too.

He had spent so much time wondering what her name was, what she did for a living, was she in fact married, did she have kids, and most importantly, would she be interested in giving him a chance. She was in front of him again and he had no intention of letting the moment pass without introducing himself to her.

He looked around to see if his best friend, Damon, had made it to the race yet, but he couldn't spot him anywhere. He wouldn't have a wing man this time around, but he wasn't going to blow his chance with meeting her. "Excuse me. Excuse me. Excuse me. Excuse me." He made his way through the crowd over to her.

He came shoulder to shoulder with her. The music from her headphones blared, letting him know the exact song she was playing. He smiled noting that she was a Janelle Monae fan just like him. He drew in a deep breath trying to take in more of her scent. She smelled good. It was some type of sporty perfume, but he was certain that it mixed well with her natural scent making her smell so invigorating to him.

He bobbed his head along to the new song that was playing in her ears. He wanted her attention so he cleared his throat loudly.

She looked over to him and gave him a somewhat friendly smile then turned her attention back to the pavement and continued to nod her head.

He smiled realizing he would have to speak up soon to engage her before the race got underway. He waved his hand out in front of her face trying to get her attention. "Hello."

She took her left ear bud out and looked in his direction. "Hello." Her eyebrows raised.

"How are you doing?"

She continued nodding her head to the music playing in her right ear. "I'm fine."

She tried to put her left ear bud back in but he kept talking. "Good. I see you run a lot."

"Hunh?" Her eyebrows furrowed. She stepped away to get a better look at him.

"I've seen you before at a few runs."

"Oh." Her facial features relaxed.

"Yeah, I've wanted to speak to you before, I just never had the chance to."

She remained silent.

Tough nut to crack. "By the way, my name is Aaron. May I ask what's yours?" He extended his arm out to shake her hand.

She stared at his hand for a second before finally gripping it. "Melanie." She let go quickly feeling an unfamiliar warmth to his touch. She looked up at him again and realized how handsome he was.

"Melanie." He said her name slowly. "I like that, Melanie." He smiled and nodded his head.

She folded her arms at her chest.

"So Melanie, how long have you been running?"

"I ran track a little in high school, but I've been consistent with running for exercise for about five years. I just recently started to run in races. It seems like race day runs really clear my mind. What about you?" The more she looked at him, the more she became intrigued with him. *Melanie, stop it. I have no business being attracted to this guy. I'm not ready to date, and besides, he's a white guy.* Melanie shook her head at her last thought.

"Yeah, I ran track in high school, too. Got a scholarship for it for college, but I run for fun now. Great cardio, too."

"I wouldn't have pegged you as a runner had I not saw you here."

"And why is that?"

"Because you have the build of a football player."

Aaron grinned. "Yeah, I get asked often if I do or did play football."

"Yeah, I can see that." She tried to put her ear bud back in her ear hoping to end the conversation with him and quell the strangeness going on in her stomach.

"So, do you run alone all of the time?"

She huffed before speaking. "No. My best friend and I run together some mornings, but I've been doing these races by myself since her schedule is really hectic."

"Okay. Well, if you've signed up for a lot of races this year and you want someone to run with, just let me know."

"Thanks, but like I said, running is one of the only times during the day where my head is clear and I desperately need the time alone." She looked and saw how defeated he appeared. "Sorry."

He held his hands loosely behind his back. "It's cool. I understand. You like to run alone and I see you constantly trying to tune me out with your music."

"No, it's not like that," Melanie said, seeking reconciliation. She shifted her body weight from one leg to the other.

"No, I totally get it, but can I have your number? Maybe I can call you after the race? That's if you don't already have a man." He raised one eyebrow at her.

She snarled. "No, I don't have a man." *Of course, I don't have a man. He turned out to be my brother.* She shuddered. She made large circles with her arms working to release the tension that had built in her shoulders at the question.

"Okay then." His eyes shifted from her to other focal points in the crowd. He didn't know what he said so bad that set her off.

"I'm sorry, I didn't mean to snap on you, it's just that—"

"No, you don't have to explain anything to me. I'm intruding on your personal space and time, asking questions that maybe I shouldn't ask."

"No, you're fine."

"Am I fine enough for you to give me your number?" He smirked staring at her.

"Um..." She shrugged her shoulders half-heartedly. "I guess."

"You guess?" His voice raised a pitch as his eyebrows raised at her.

Their shoulders bounced up and down as they let out hearty laughs.

"Well, I'm not afraid to admit how beautiful I think you are." He stared at her hoping not to make her any more uncomfortable than she appeared to be seeing as though she was shifting from one foot to the other with her head down.

She blushed and turned her face away from him trying to regain her composure. Sensing that he was staring at her, she finally turned her face back towards him. "Thanks."

"But you still didn't say if I was fine to you?" He chuckled.

Melanie smiled. "Whatever. I'm not answering that."

"That's okay, you don't have to. I'm okay as long as I get to see that smile of yours." He was glad that she had her phone out from her armband and was switching the songs. The act allowed him to gently pull her phone out of her hand and store his number in it.

***

Damon stood out of view in the same corral as Aaron.

He had gotten there later than what he told Aaron he would. He searched for Aaron until he spotted him talking to the fine sista he had planned on talking to the next time he saw her at a race. He never had the chance to catch up to her. She was as beautiful that day as the other two times he saw her at races. He had a feeling she had her stuff together and he wanted a woman like her instead of the ones that seemed to gravitate to him hoping that he would finance their ghetto dreams of keeping their hair and nails done and wearing the latest fashions. He wanted more with and from a woman, and he was certain he could have that with her, even though he knew nothing about her.

His deep-brown skin tightened over his jaws as he clenched them together. He grinded his teeth. The muscles in his well-defined biceps and triceps flexed as he opened and closed his fists. He was pissed as he watched Aaron talking to her and how he was making her laugh. *Her smile. It's beautiful. I should be the one to make her smile like that, not Aaron.*

Aaron had been his boy since middle school; they were like brothers, but he always hated how Aaron seemed to get all the women that he wanted, the good, black girls.

But she, whoever she was, would be his this time.

The announcer signaled the start of the race but he didn't walk over to greet Aaron. He needed time to think.

8

Dear Diary,

Well, it's time to unload in you again. If I'm not spilling my guts with you, I'm either pushing my thoughts aside as I run, or burying myself in my paintings at the gallery. Sometimes I wish you could talk back to me, but then again, if you could you'd probably push me to reconcile sooner with my mom and Andrew like they and my dad do often. I really love my dad and I normally enjoy talking to him and spending time with him, but since he's been nagging me, too, about really talking to my mom about keeping Andrew a secret, I've had to ignore him, too. Seems like the only people I can tolerate talking to nowadays are Aaron and Karen, when she's not busy working or with Kyle. (btw, I miss my friend). Yeah, I haven't updated you on Aaron. So, he's a guy I met at a run about three weeks ago. I really didn't want to talk to him because I'm just not ready to even think about getting serious with a guy. And there is another thing about him that makes me leery of him...he's white. I'm not racist or anything and I was only joking with Karen when I said it would probably be safer if I get with a white guy rather than chancing falling in love with another black man. I think the likelihood of me being related to a white guy is slim to none. Or is it? LOL. I'm trying my best not to like him but he's making it hard not to. He doesn't know about what happened with Andrew, my mom, and I, and I want to leave it that way for now. He's just so charming, easy to talk to, and from what I remember, definitely easy on the eyes. He's been asking if he could take me on a date since the day I met him at the race. I haven't agreed yet, but he seems pretty cool with me declining every offer. He still sends me a good morning text every morning, random cute texts through the day (that I try to pretend are not cute), and good night texts even though I had just spent hours on the phone with him. He even asked me to pray with him a few times. Now that's a first from any man I've ever dated. He owns a few shoe stores around town, so he understands what it's like to be an entrepreneur like me. If I were ready to date, a guy like him would be my top choice, a black one though. Again, I'm not racist, but I always saw myself marrying a strong, black man. Having some cute, chocolate babies. Having the model black family. I don't wanna turn my back on my brothas, I still believe in them, but then again, one of the brothas turned out to be my actual brother.

She shuddered.

"I gotta stop doing that." Melanie shook her head at herself.

Well, let me get up and get dressed. I feel like I'm starting to get back to my normal self since I've been talking to Aaron, and it feels great, even though I haven't talked to my mom and Andrew. I wonder if that has to be my new norm to continue to feel good.

Melanie pouted.

I finally get to hang out with my best friend. We're going to our favorite restaurant.

Melanie laid her pen between the pages she wrote on and closed her journal. She left it on the bed figuring she might get back to it when she got home and wanted to leave it accessible. She headed into her bathroom upbeat about seeing Karen and eating. Her appetite was back and she was ready to chow down.

***

Melanie walked into the restaurant and smiled seeing as though her regular booth in the back was open.

"Excuse me, I'd like a booth for two," she said to the hostess.

"Okay, right this way." The hostess grabbed two menus and signaled Melanie to follow her.

"Mel, I have a table already." Karen pulled on Melanie's wrist. She had just left from the bathroom.

"Hey, I didn't think you were here already. I see our table is empty. Why aren't you sitting there?" Melanie said.

They hugged.

"I wanted to switch it up a bit."

"Fine with me. Sorry, ma'am. My friend has a table for us already."

The hostess smiled and walked back to her podium.

Karen held on to Melanie's wrist and led her to their table.

Melanie was all smiles and chatting with Karen until she saw who was sitting at the table waiting on them. "Karen, why'd you invite me here knowing he would be here?" Melanie tried to walk away but Karen kept a firm grip on her wrist.

"Because if I told you, you wouldn't have come."

"You're right. And that's exactly why I'm leaving now."

"No, you're not." Karen had to dig the heel of her boots into the carpet to get her footing to keep Melanie in place.

"Oh, yes I am. I thought you were on my side." Melanie's eyes saddened.

"I am, Mel, and that's why you have to stay and talk to him. You look like you've picked some of your weight back up. You're looking good, girl. Got that glow back of yours." Karen winked at Melanie.

"Whatever." Melanie rolled her eyes.

"But he was a big part of your life, so you two need to talk, figure out how you're going to move forward." Karen walked closer to Melanie. "Even if you never accept him as your brother, which I kind of understand, he's Kyle's best friend and you're my best friend, which means that while Kyle and I are together, you two are bound to end up in the same room together. I want you two to get past this awkward stage of yours so we can move on to all of us simply being friends. Or at least existing in the same room without shuddering or wanting to run away."

Melanie cocked her head.

"Really, Mel, please do this for me. You know I love Kyle and he's Kyle's best friend. We really want our best friends around us sometimes." Karen pouted.

Melanie huffed and rolled her eyes. She had been in a good mood since she started talking to Aaron. *Maybe if I think about Aaron while I'm here I can stomach Andrew.* She looked to Karen. "Okay. I'll stay, but if I choose not to answer certain questions, please don't pressure me, because I will walk out and leave your scheming tail here."

"Thanks best friend." Karen jovially air kissed both of Melanie's cheeks.

Melanie curled her lip in a snarl and wiped off the imaginary kisses. "And you owe me big time."

"You bet." Karen pulled on Melanie's wrist as she walked ahead to the table.

Kyle and Andrew stood when they saw the ladies finally walk up to the table.

"Is everything okay?" Kyle asked.

"Yeah, everything is okay," Karen said.

"Melanie, it's been a minute since I've seen you. You look great." Kyle extended his arms to hug Melanie.

She accepted his hug. She was happy Karen ended up with Kyle instead of Dennis.

"Melanie," Andrew uttered, wondering how much he could say to her before she shut him down as she did the last time he saw her.

The guys each held one of the ladies chairs out for them.

Karen sat down as Kyle tucked her chair in under her.

"Andrew." Melanie barely acknowledged him. "I can get my own chair, thanks."

Andrew shook his head.

Karen smiled as Kyle kissed her on her cheek.

Melanie buried her head in the menu pretending like she needed to look it over, but since she had been there so many times before with Karen and Andrew, she knew it like the scars on the back of her hand.

"So, Mel, how are things going down at the art gallery?" Kyle asked, trying to stir up a conversation.

"Great." She never looked up from the menu.

"So, did you restock your inventory with that new artist's pieces you wanted?" Andrew asked as he closed his menu. He already knew what he wanted.

Melanie didn't respond to Andrew.

Karen kicked Melanie under the table.

Melanie's nostrils flared and she shot Karen a look letting her know she better not test her.

Karen smiled politely, but not genuinely at her.

Andrew huffed. He turned to Melanie. "Look, Mel, neither one of us asked to be each other's brother and sister, but we are, so deal with it."

Melanie slowly turned her head to Andrew.

Karen held her breath hoping the 'sista souljah' didn't come out of Melanie. For as calm and collect as Melanie could be, she did have a fierce streak in her that took no prisoners if need be.

Kyle laughed under his breath. He couldn't believe Andrew said what he said to Melanie, but he admitted to himself that it was the truth.

Andrew stared Melanie in her eyes ready for whatever she had to say to him.

She angled her entire body towards him before speaking. "So how do you propose we move forward, Andrew?" She laced her fingers together and rested one elbow on the table and the other across the back of her chair as she awaited his response.

Karen's eyes widened. "Wait, that's your response to him?"

Kyle squeezed Karen's hand. "Karen, let's stay out of this unless we absolutely have to run interference."

"Well, Melanie, trust that I understand how you're feeling. I was right there with you, feeling the same feelings you were."

Karen and Melanie shuddered.

"What?" Kyle asked.

"Nothing." Karen responded to him.

Andrew furrowed his eyebrows giving the ladies a quizzical look before he continued. "It was hard on me, not to mention weird, finding out that the woman I was in love with was actually my sister."

Karen and Melanie shuddered again.

"But you of all people should know how I longed for my birth mother and how much I wanted to get to know her and any other brothers and sisters I may have. So while I can understand that things may be weird between us for a while, I won't ignore you when I see you as you do me. I want to have a relationship with you as my sister. I can respect that that will take time to develop, but because you are my sister, we will have a sibling relationship," Andrew stated matter-of-factly as he stared at Melanie.

"Well, you just told me why you want us to get along, but you didn't tell me *how* you expect us to get along as sister and brother in contrast to being who we once were to each other." Melanie raised one eyebrow to Andrew. Her phone alerted her that she had a text message. She pulled it out of her purse and read the message on the screen while Karen, Kyle, and Andrew looked on waiting to see what would happen next.

Melanie giggled as she responded to Aaron texts.

The light from her screen casted a glow on her face. She slowly looked up at the others at the table sensing the eerie silence around her. "What?"

"What? Are you serious? You're in the middle of a very interesting and much needed conversation with your brother," Karen shuddered, "and you pull out your phone all giddy and text."

Melanie laughed. "So. I'm allowed to text on the phone I pay the bill on."

Andrew rested his head on his fist as he stared at Melanie.

Melanie looked over him. "What, you got something to say, too?"

Andrew remained speechless.

"You," Melanie looked at Karen, "and you," she looked at Andrew, "basically told me that I have to come to terms with the way things turned out between my *brother* and I," she shortened her shudder, but looked over to see Karen shiver, "then that's what I'm doing." She looked back down at her phone smiling and sent another text to Aaron.

"I've seen that look in your eyes before," Andrew said and scooted his chair back so he could get a better look at Melanie.

"What look?" Karen cocked her head at Melanie. She lifted herself out of her chair, reached across the table, and snatched Melanie's phone out of her hand.

"Karen, give me my phone back now," Melanie demanded.

"No. I wanna know what and who shifted you into a good mood so quickly."

"I'll tell you later. Now give me my phone back."

An incoming text lit up Melanie's screen.

Karen read it. "Aaron? Who is Aaron? He kept you up all last night on the phone? He can't wait to take you out?" Karen tried to read the rest of the text but Melanie was now out of her seat and had snatched her phone back from Karen.

"I told you I would tell you later, nosey. You talk too much." Melanie opened her mouth to criticize Karen for badgering her about Aaron in front of the men, but she closed her mouth and focused her attention back on her phone.

The waiter came and took their orders.

Melanie continued to text while everyone stared at her after the waiter left.

"So is that why you put the lion back in the cage on me real quick?" Andrew said.

Melanie raised her eyebrows at him.

"I mean calmed down the venom you were about to spit at me. Some other guy has your attention already?"

"What's it matter to you, *brother*?"

Karen and Kyle eyed each other in disbelief before returning their attention back to Andrew and Melanie.

"Thank you for acknowledging that I am your brother."

Kyle pressed his lips together trying to suppress his laughter. While the subject matter was reprehensible, the body language and verbal sparring between the duo was hysterical in action.

"And as your brother, it's my responsibility to protect you. I don't think it's healthy for you to get involved with someone so soon after us."

Karen shuddered.

Melanie laughed.

Kyle kicked Andrew under the table.

Melanie turned completely towards Andrew again. She zoomed her stare in on him.

Karen just knew she would have to come to Andrew's rescue this time.

Melanie said, "Well, brother, I was taking care of myself looooong before you came along and whether or not we eeevvveeer become close as siblings, I'll still be able to take care of myself. And remember, since we are just brother and sister, I don't have a single romantic bone or feeling for you in my body. What we had in that way, is so in the past. Now leave it there." With beady eyes, Melanie slowly turned her attention back towards Karen. She mouthed to Karen. "I'm going to get you."

Karen pretended like she couldn't read Melanie's lips. "Well, since we're no longer living in the past, let's discuss the present and the possible future. I know you said you would tell me later, but since it's out in the open now you might as well tell us all about him. I mean we are all friends, right?"

Everyone looked to Melanie awaiting her response.

"Yeah." She granted them a fake smile.

Karen and Kyle exchange knowing looks with one another.

Andrew's face remained stoic.

"So tell us." Karen prodded Melanie.

"There's nothing to tell. I met him at a run and we've been talking and texting ever since."

Melanie looked down at her phone smiling while reading Aaron's most recent text he had sent her.

"Mel!" Karen demanded her attention.

"Hold on." Melanie didn't look up at Karen until she finished texting her response to Aaron.

"Mel, give me the phone." Karen wiggled her fingers with her palm facing up waiting for Melanie to give her the phone.

"Alright, alright, alright. I'll put it away, but let me send this last text."

Karen rolled her eyes at Melanie.

Melanie giggled as she typed then pressed send. She secured her phone in her purse as the waiter started placing each of their entrees in front of them.

"Let's hold hands and say grace," Andrew said.

Melanie was hesitant to hold Andrew's hand, so she positioned her hand so he would only be able to grab her fingertips.

Karen shook her head noting the quiet dispute between Andrew and Melanie. She lowered her head and mumbled to herself. "Well, they're already starting to act like brother and sister."

Kyle heard Karen and a wide grin stretched across his face. He loved her sense of humor.

Andrew said a quick prayer and Melanie was quick to pull back the little of her hand he held.

"Okay, so tell us about him." Karen egged Melanie to talk.

"Karen, she'll tell you about him when she's ready," Kyle said.

Karen shot a 'shut your mouth' look at Kyle.

He said no more.

Melanie was in a happy mood after her quick texting convo with Aaron. She reasoned that since Karen might tell Kyle about Aaron anyway who would in turn tell Andrew, she might as well tell them all together. She finished chewing before she said, "As I said before, there's nothing to tell. I met him at a run and we've been talking and texting one another ever since."

"What kind of man just texts a woman like you?" Andrew asked. He hadn't touched his food yet.

"The kind of man that respects that woman's wishes," Melanie snapped back.

Karen and Kyle fell against one another whimpering their laughter.

"What?" Andrew and Melanie asked consecutively.

"You two are pretty good at this brother-sister thing already," Kyle said.

"You know, the whole at odds with one another brother-sister type relationship," Karen followed up Kyle's comment.

"Oh whatever." Melanie stuck more of her food in her mouth.

Andrew bit into a breadstick. "I'm just saying, if a man is serious about a woman, he would do more than simply text and call her," Andrew griped.

"Again, a man who respects a woman's wishes would settle for that in the meantime. Like you said, *brother,* I have no business jumping into anything serious." Melanie pursed her lips at Andrew.

He gave her a straight face like he didn't believe her. "So what does he do for a living?"

"Dang, *brother,* you all up in my business." Melanie snickered.

"Stop saying *brother* like that," Andrew said.

"Like what?" Melanie swallowed her laughter and kept her lips tight together.

"Answer the question. What does he do for a living?"

"He owns a few shoe stores around town?"

"Selling what kind of shoes?" Kyle jumped in.

"His stores cater to all kinds of men's shoes, from gym shoes to wing tip dress shoes."

"Mmhh." Karen smirked. "A business man."

"What kind of family does he come from?" Andrew asked, flaring his nostrils.

Melanie looked at Karen. "Karen, or better yet, Kyle," she looked at Kyle, "will you tell my *brother* that I am no longer answering any of his questions." She put more food into her mouth.

Kyle, hysterical with laughter, gasped for air while Karen drummed her feet against the floor letting her laughter course through her body. Melanie's responses and body language towards Andrew was giving her life. She remembered back to how brash she used to be with shooting down Kyle's constant pursuit of her. So for her to have a front row seat to Melanie dismissing Andrew was reminiscently amusing.

Andrew shook his head.

"Okay, you didn't answer it when Andrew asked it, but I want to know to. What kind of family does he come from?" Kyle jumped in.

Melanie put her fork down. "Why does that even matter? I'm certain his can't be any more screwed up than mine is."

Kyle gave Melanie the "sorry we asked" look.

Andrew said, "What happened with Mom was tragic and a one-time deal. His family, he could be doing illegal things to date. How do you even know he got those stores the legal way? If he owns as many stores as you say that he does then Kyle and I should've heard of him, met him at the Black Businessmen League meetings at some point or another."

"Who said he was black?" Melanie cut her eyes at Andrew and sipped on her water.

Karen's eyes widened. "What? I thought you were joking about our conversation the other day. Are you seriously dating a white guy?" Karen freed her hands of utensils and locked them together under her chin giving her full attention to Melanie.

Kyle wiped his mouth of any Alfredo sauce and sat quietly waiting for Melanie's response.

Andrew angled his body towards Melanie waiting for her response.

Melanie ignored Kyle's and Andrew's stares and directed her response to Karen. "What? It's not like I went looking for him; he approached me. He's a great guy from what I've gathered thus far."

Karen squeaked. "So when are you two going out?"

"I didn't say we were."

"Why not? If he's a great guy like you say he is and he's a business owner, he seems like a good catch. I think you should give him a chance," Karen said.

"I admit talking to him has helped my mood these past couple of weeks. He's kind of helping me get back to my old self, but as far as dating him, I'm not sure about that."

"Why not?" Karen asked confused.

"Well, because he's…"

"He's what?" Karen asked.

Melanie leaned in closer to Karen. "Because he's white."

Karen grinned. "Duh."

Kyle jumped into the conversation. "Good."

"And what is that supposed to mean?" Karen asked Kyle with a stern look on her face.

"I'm just saying, I don't think white guys really know how to treat black women. I think they just want y'all for your curves. I think they look at y'all like you're just some aphrodisiac."

Melanie looked at Karen and said, "Should I take this one or you?"

Karen replied, "How about I start off and you fill in as need be."

Andrew shook his head and lifted his hands in surrender as he backed up from the table when Kyle gave him the "help me out" look.

Karen narrowed her eyes in on Kyle.

"What?" Kyle asked, smirking at Karen.

She was quick to respond to him. "Don't what me. For as many women of different races that you've slept with, hell the mother of your child, Mercedes, is Brazilian, I wouldn't think that you would fix your mouth, let alone your thoughts, to have an issue with someone dating outside of their race."

Melanie high-fived Karen.

Andrew continued to shake his head as if suggesting he wanted no part of the conversation.

"All I'm saying is that it's different when a black man dates a white woman or any other woman outside of his race than when a black woman dates a man outside of her race. That's all I'm saying." Kyle hoped that would dim the spotlight on him.

"Please explain why, sir," Melanie said.

Kyle looked to Andrew again for help.

"You're on your own on this one buddy," Andrew responded.

"You finally said something smart for a change tonight." Melanie looked at Andrew.

Andrew smirked at Melanie.

Kyle sat up straight. He knew Karen was feisty and quick on her toes. He didn't want what he might say to start an argument with her that he would have to make up for later. All of the chatter and clanking of utensils against dishes at nearby tables seemed to fade out as Kyle sat contemplating what to say next.

Karen stared at him as he paused. "No, don't hold back. Learning what you think about this topic is good intel for me."

"What? You're doing an interview on me. You're not going to try and use what I say here against me on your show, are you? You're my girlfriend tonight, not the great Karen Roberts, host of the hottest sports show nationally syndicated and a Bulls correspondent."

Karen wore a sly grin. "Of course not, honey." She caressed his face. "I just want to know why you think what you think."

Kyle looked at Andrew.

"You might as well tell the truth, because from the looks of her demeanor, you're gonna pay for it anyway." Andrew laughed as he rested his elbow on the table.

Kyle pretended to wipe sweat from his forehead as he cleared his throat to speak. "In my opinion, when a white man seeks out a black woman, he's trying to see what makes her so different than a white woman, you know, get the inside scoop on why her hair is so curly, why her butt is so big, enjoy her cooking, and things like that. She's more of a conquest for him. Sad to say, but it's kind of like how slave masters snuck around with the black women during slave times."

Karen bit her tongue.

Melanie stared at Karen waiting to see how she would respond. When Karen remained silent, she gave her attention back to Kyle.

"But when a black man gets with a white woman, in general, and equally sad to say, it's because he hasn't had any luck with a black woman. A white woman seems to know how to let a man lead. She respects him and really ladies, that's all a man wants, is to be respected."

Karen scrunched her face up. She cocked her head and looked to Melanie. "Did you just hear the same thing I heard?"

Melanie contorted her face in bewilderment. "Yes."

"I mean did he really just say what he said?" Karen was dumbfounded.

Melanie nodded her head. "Yes."

Karen backed her chair up, putting an arm's length distance between her and Kyle. She looked him up and down. She shook her head in between her open hands. "So you're telling me that when it comes to dating outside of their race, a black woman gets looked at as an object to be investigated, but when a white woman gets picked by a black man, it's because she's treasured and appreciated?"

"I'm not saying everyone thinks like that, but in most, many cases, whether they want to admit it or not, yes, they do."

"Kyle, I thought I knew you. I thought you were smarter than this." Karen shook her head in disbelief.

Kyle raised an eyebrow at Karen.

Karen pulled her chair back up to the table and looked to Andrew and Melanie. She refused to look at Kyle anymore. "You idiots, many black men that is, especially you athletes and stars, don't understand that when that white woman comes at you all humble and docile, that's because she sees that you're about to cash in on your talent, so she lures you into her with this false sense of submission to you. Yeah, she'll play the role of doing whatever it is that you want her to and you're comforted into not signing a pre-nup. She loves that because she knows at some point the stardom will get to your head and you'll screw up big time cheating on her and whatnot. Then, when she asks for that divorce, you'll be forced to pay her royally in alimony plus loads of money in child support because she had no problem popping out as many of your kids as you wanted her to. She knew that each of them would add to her bottom line when the time came to cash in on you."

Kyle tried to interrupt Karen but she silenced him with one finger and a threatening stare.

"Melanie, is there anything you'd like to add?"

"Well, I think you just did a fine job explaining that and I know you could continue on, but yes I'd like to jump in and speak on behalf of my strong, black sisters."

Kyle took in a deep breath and let it out slowly.

"See Kyle, and maybe this is for you too Andrew, because I remember you telling me that you dated outside of your race. When it comes to black women, you all loathe because you think they have funky attitudes and don't know how to be submissive, what you don't pay attention to closely about them is what they have to endure. You think it's hard being a black man because of the way society labels you all as thugs no matter how great your accomplishments may be, but I think black women have it harder because not only do we face sexism on our jobs, we have to deal with your ish. We're there to support you through it all. Jail time, college graduations, no matter what. We take care of the kids, work, and go to school trying to help and take some of the burden off your shoulders, but when you all make it big, the first thing you all do is snatch up a white woman to parade around in the spotlight as if she's the trophy, the pinnacle of your success. It seems as if you all forget all that we sacrificed to help you achieve your dreams. You objectify us as mere sex objects but you all are quick to elevate them as the epitome of a woman. Our attitudes come from being pushed aside by society and thinking that our black brothers will be our safe haven only to find out that you all are so quick to treat us like dirt like everyone else has been doing. We ride so hard for you all, but you all drop us as soon as you sign on the dotted line. Now while I may be apprehensive about dating a white guy, my stomach is more calmed by seeing a white guy with a black woman, than seeing a black man with a white woman. And on that note, I'm out of here, y'all. This was a very interesting dinner, but I'm ready to go now." She looked at Andrew. "*Brother,* why don't you be a good big *brother* and cover my meal." She smirked at him, gathered her belongings, and looked at Karen as she finished her speech. "I'll talk to you later."

She left.

9

Melanie sat in the soul food restaurant wondering whether or not she was actually doing the right thing by meeting Aaron there. She laughed as she sat at a table near a window at the front of the restaurant thinking of how she chose that restaurant of all places to have a date with him.

She had rushed home from dinner the other night, boggled by Kyle sharing his asinine ideology on genders dating outside of their race. The more she thought about it, she wasn't totally sure about being out with Aaron, let alone dating again, but with enjoying their conversations on the phone, she was curious to know if she would enjoy his face to face company.

"Cute shirt," the woman at a nearby table called out to her.

"Thanks." She smiled at the woman and looked down at her 'black girls rock' shirt. *Am I being a hypocrite? Or is it really that love knows no color?*

A flood of questions of whether or not being there was right for her streamed through her mind.

She grabbed her purse and got up to leave but walked right into Aaron.

"Hey you." He smiled at her. "You weren't about to leave me hanging here, were you?" He noticed the uncertainty in her eyes.

"Uh, uh, uh…" She patted her big, curly hair nervously. "No, I wasn't."

"You sure?"

"I'm sure."

"Okay, so let's sit down then."

He was chivalrous in pushing her chair in under her as she sat back down at the table. He handed her the bouquet of calla lilies she had been oblivious to him holding when she walked into him.

She looked down at the floral arrangement and smiled as she took them from him. "I love these. These are my favorite. Thank you."

"I know." He grinned as he sat down.

"How'd you know?" She raised one eyebrow.

"I remember everything you've ever told me about you."

"Oh." She blushed.

He looked around the restaurant. "So I take it that this is one of your favorite spots?"

"Yeah, it is."

"Cool, if it's your favorite, I'm certain it'll become mine."

Melanie looked up to see the same woman that complimented her on her shirt earlier now snarling at her.

"Is everything okay?" Aaron asked Melanie.

"Yeah." She feigned a smile.

A waiter came over to their table to take their order. He looked to Melanie first. "Do you know what you'd like, sista? Because it clearly ain't brothas." He mumbled the last of his statement low hoping they wouldn't hear him.

"Excuse me?" Melanie stared at him with a raised eyebrow.

"I asked if you knew what you wanted from the menu." He smiled trying to smooth things over with her.

She took a deep breath and looked back down at her menu. She'd heard what he said. She kind of expected the looks and comments she was now getting from others around the restaurant. Oddly, she chose going to that restaurant to see how it would be being out in public with Aaron. She didn't like it so far.

She looked up at the waiter. "I'll have the jerk chicken with greens and sweet potatoes."

"Okay." The waiter started walking away.

"Wait, aren't you going to take his order?" Melanie asked with a look of confusion.

"Oh yeah." He walked back to the table. "Do you know what you want? All we have here is soul food." He looked at Aaron.

"Um, we know that. That's why we're here."

"My bad." The waiter looked at Melanie.

"You know what," Melanie stood up toe to toe with the waiter, "I need to speak to your manager." Her nostrils flared.

"Melanie." Aaron called her name softly forcing her to calm her stance and look to him. He stared into her eyes and smiled. "It's okay." He then looked at the waiter. "I was practically raised on soul food, so I know what I want. I'll have fried chicken with spaghetti, corn on the cob, and corn bread."

"Well, alrighty then. I'll be back in a minute with some water to get you all started." The waiter pivoted and left their table.

Aaron looked at Melanie. He reached out and grabbed her hand across the table coercing her to sit down. She obliged him. He slowly caressed the back of her balled fist with his thumb trying to calm her down. Judging from her still flared nostrils and heavy breathing, he could tell she was mad. "Melanie, whatever it is, let it go."

"Let it go? Let it go? You don't see what's going on around here?"

He knew what she was hinting at but he wanted to ignore it. "What?" He laughed and leaned back in his chair.

"Oh this is no laughing matter. Before you came in here, they were all smiles directed at me, but since you've sat down across from me, there's been nothing but dirty stares, lip smacking, eye rolling, and the waiter had the nerve to almost refuse you service. I think we should leave."

"No, we don't have to. If this is somewhere you want to be, then we'll be here."

"I don't want to be here if they won't respect who I'm with. I had a feeling it might be like this. I should've never come here." She pulled her hand from his grasp, folded her arms at her chest, and tapped her foot as she stared out the window at nothing in particular.

"Be like what? And do you mean you shouldn't have come to the place or just not out with me?" He leaned into the table and laced his hands together staring intently at her.

She finally looked at him as she had the feeling he was staring at her. She wanted to stay seething with anger, but when she looked at him, he was just so darn cute to her that a slow smile crept across her face as his alluring eyes softened her. She scooted back up to the table. "Look, Aaron, I don't know if you've noticed it or not, but I'm black and you're white."

"You don't say." He feigned a look of shock.

"Whatever." She rolled her eyes and laughed. "I'm being serious here. I know it's 2015, but it seems like this country is still as racist and as prejudicial as it was from its inception."

He nodded solemnly.

"I've told you during one of our talks that I wasn't sure if I was ready to date again, but to have to add being discriminated against and whatnot to a relationship, I don't think I'm ready for that. I mean these stares and the way he treated you, that doesn't bother you?"

He rubbed his chin readying himself to respond to her.

The waiter returned with their drinks. He quickly placed them on the table and scurried off noting Melanie's combative stare at him.

Aaron was cleared his throat. "In 2015, do I think that there's something wrong with people still being racist? Yes. Do I wish that wasn't the case? Desperately. Will I let it stop me from dating who I want to date? No. As I told you before, I've only ever dated black women. And not because I'm trying to be down or think I'm one of the brothas. I can only be me, and this here white man loves black women. I told you I was raised in a mixed neighborhood. My best friends were black when I was growing up, my godmomma is black, and I was over her house all the time, so of course I'm familiar and comfortable with a lot of black traditions and whatnot. I love black culture."

Melanie pursed her lips studying Aaron's sincerity. The genuineness in his eyes momentarily suspended her fears of giving him a chance. She smiled at him.

"I know that I will never know what it's like to be black in America, but if you never give us a chance, you'll never know what it's like to be with Aaron Oliver." He popped his collar and laughed.

"Oh whatever." She playfully rolled her eyes at him as a grin slowly covered her face. She felt so calm whenever she focused solely on him.

"So since you've only ever dated black women, how do you deal with the racism?" Melanie frowned.

"Do you let, let's say another art gallery dictate what paintings you will put up in your gallery?"

"No." Melanie snapped.

"So, that's kind of how I deal with it. I know who I am. And then I know what I want and I go from there. As long as no one brings any physical harm to my lady, myself, or any of my physical property, then what they say or do doesn't matter to me. It's that simple to me."

"Well, it's not that simple to me."

"It can be."

"Like you said, because you don't know what it's like to be black, you don't know what we deal with when it comes to interracial dating."

"And neither do you since I'm your first. Unless you've been dating my brothers for years but won't admit it." He looked at her suspiciously as one of his eyebrows raised.

"Oh whatever. You're my first."

"I would love to be your one and only." He pretended to cough as he covered his mouth and said his next words, "Shoot, the man you spend the rest of your life with."

Melanie leaned over the table. "What did you say?"

"Oh nothing." He laughed.

"Yeah, right." She smirked at him.

"Seriously, if you're really uncomfortable we can leave, but if not, we'll sit here and enjoy this food you seem to love. Honestly, at this point, I don't care what's going on around me as long as I'm able to look at you. Be in your presence."

Melanie fidgeted with her purse under the table. Aaron's stare strengthened the more he gazed at her. She needed to cool off from him. "You know, I ain't no punk, but I won't patronize a place who would be so blatantly discriminatory. I want to leave."

"Well then, we'll leave."

Melanie raised her hand signaling for help.

The waiter made his way over to her.

"I would like to speak to your manager."

"I am the manager."

"Good to know. Well, you know as well as I know that it was inappropriate how you ignored my date when taking my order and I heard the comment you made. We don't want to eat here, so we're leaving."

"Ma'am, I apologize if I offended you earlier. How about you stay and enjoy your meal for free on me."

"See, you're still doing it. You have yet to address my date. He's the one you're disrespecting and you're just trying to smooth things over so I won't leave some type of bad review via social media or something. But please know that I plan to. The rest of the world should know what kind of racist establishment you run." Melanie stood up and Aaron slowly followed suit.

"Ma'am, I'm sorry. Is there anything I can do to make up for earlier?"

"Yes."

The guy smiled in relief. "What can I do?"

"Get out of my way." Melanie extended her hand out to Aaron.

He grabbed it gently and rested his other hand on the small of her back as he escorted her out of the restaurant.

"Let me walk you to your car."

"Uh duh. You better." She laughed a little, easing some of the tension her grand exit from the restaurant created.

They both laughed as Aaron held onto her hand and she led him to her car. He stood near her on the driver's side.

"Despite what happened in there, I really enjoyed being able to see you in the flesh as we talked, rather than settling for phone convos and texts." Aaron winked at her.

"Yeah, looking back, being with you made that nasty experience much more tolerable."

"I wish we had more time together tonight," Aaron said.

"I know, right? I like picking your brain."

"I like it when you do that, too."

She playfully hit him on his arm.

He grabbed her hand and pulled it close to his mouth. He pecked on the back of her hand.

Melanie took a deep breath noting how soft Aaron's lips were on her skin. His closeness to her made her not want their night to end just yet. "Look, I don't normally invite guys back to my house so soon, but sense you seem harmless—" She playfully stared him up and down.

"I am." He smiled, interrupting her.

"How about we go back to my place? We didn't eat, and I'm starving. We can order pizza and just talk."

"You know we don't have to go back to your place if you're not comfortable with that. There are plenty of pizza places open late into the night. I just want you to be comfortable."

She smiled. "Thanks. I just don't want to go somewhere else and we experience that same ignorance. We definitely would avoid that at my place."

"Are you sure?"

"Yup. And besides, if you do try something with me, I have something at my place to protect me."

Aaron stepped back from her. "Should I be scared?"

"Depends," Melanie said.

10

It was another season with the Bulls and Kyle had been moved to the small forward position, seeing as though the former small forward was traded to another team right before the season began. The trade didn't bother Kyle, team management, or his teammates one bit because Kyle had proven himself to be extremely valuable to the team last year, even though they didn't win the championship.

With the way Kyle looked in practices over the summer, the whole team was happy for him to be in his new position and so was Karen. She knew how much he wanted a ring this season and his new position was bound to make that happen.

A game was underway as Karen sat on the sidelines broadcasting with her cohost. "I gotta tell you, Stacey, the Bulls are looking like they're ready to take the title this year." Karen smiled as she talked into her microphone and looked at Stacey.

"Yeah, I can definitely say the same. Hot sauce!" Stacey blurted out as Kirk Heinrich drained a three with two seconds left on the shot clock. Stacey smiled looking back at Karen. "Yeah, we're only four games into the season, but with this rotation of players that Hoiberg has in place, and the new offensive mindset of the team, we're definitely coming out victorious out of the western conference finals."

"*We* are?" Karen laughed.

"Yes, we. I will forever be a Bull," Stacey said, reminiscing on his days as a Chicago Bulls player.

Karen shrugged her shoulders. "I guess."

"Okay, let's focus back on the game."

"Yes, and we're just in time because Kyle Irving has once again stolen the ball from the Grizzlies point guard and is headed back down court in what I predict will be an uncontested slam dunk." Karen beamed with pride watching her man make his way down the court with such determination to score. She frowned looking at the venomous face of the Grizzlies point guard on Kyle's heels.

Kyle dribbled as fast as he could realizing the point guard was right behind him. He didn't want to chance a layup and miss. He wanted a slam dunk that would surely earn him a poster picture for the night's game.

Adrenaline flowing forcefully through his body, Kyle quickened his steps as Bulls fans cheered him on loudly. His eyes locked in on the rim as he soared in the air for the slam dunk.

Still seated fans jumped to their feet and the crowd roared as Kyle's dunk electrified the arena.

Kyle hung from the rim for quite some time before he jumped down and landed on his butt. His adrenaline was still racing heavily through his body rendering him clueless as to why the reporters and those seated at the baseline gasped and covered their mouths.

The cameras zoomed in on his leg and displayed it on the big screen.

There was complete silence in the arena. Kyle couldn't understand why it was so quiet after his great display of athleticism during his dunk. His breathing slowed down as he finally tried to get up from the floor to no avail. Still clueless as to why the crowd was silent, Kyle looked up at the big screen before he tried to get up again. His eyes widened as he quickly looked back at his right leg to see that his bone had ripped through his skin.

He wanted to reach out and grab his leg as the pain now began to register to his brain, but by that time, the team's doctors huddled around him.

"Kyle, stop moving. Just lay back. We have this." The head doctor for the team knelt beside Kyle.

Kyle screamed out expletives as he tried to rock from side to side hoping it would alleviate the piercing pain permeating his leg.

"Oh my God." Karen jumped up and tore away the mics connected to her.

Stacey pulled on her arm as he turned his mic off. "Karen, I know that you two are together and you want to go see about him now—"

"Yes. I have to. He's hurt. I have to go be with him." Karen tried pulling away from Stacey.

He gently held on tightly to her. "I know, Karen, but remember you are reporting this game now and we're live. We have to finish this." Stacey stared into Karen's eyes hoping that she would see the sincerity and compassion they held for her current dilemma.

She wiped the tears from her face realizing that Stacey was right. She was at work and she needed to do her job. She *had* to finish covering the game, but her heart left on the stretcher with Kyle.

***

Karen sat alongside Kyle's parents, Mercedes, and Gabrielle in the waiting area outside of the operating room. Although she held her breath waiting for the surgeons to come out and tell them the severity of Kyle's injuries, she couldn't help but to stare at Gabrielle with mixed emotions. Gabrielle had become the source of Kyle's greatest joy, but she was becoming the thorn in her side.

Karen shook her head hoping to free her mind of looking at Gabrielle in any negative manner. Gabby, as everyone called her, was a little girl who had no control over how she came into the world and who her parents were. She couldn't help that she wanted to spend as much time as she could with her daddy when he was in town.

Karen was lost in thought when the doctor came out of the operating room. She didn't know what was going on around her until she looked to where Kyle's father once sat next to her and saw that the chair was empty. She looked up to see everyone crowding around the doctor.

She rushed over to join his family.

Kyle's father moved over allowing her to see the doctor's face. He draped his arm over her shoulder and squeezed it hoping to calm her trembling body.

"Mr. and Mrs. Irving?"

"Yes?" Kyle's mother said holding back her tears.

"Kyle is fine and we were successful with putting his bone back in place and suturing up his skin."

"Oh thank God!" Kyle's mom threw her hands up in the air, and then wrapped her arms around her husband's waist. "Praise God."

"So how soon will he be able to get back on the court?" Kyle's father asked, knowing that would be exactly what Kyle wanted to know.

The surgeon took a deep breath before speaking. "Mr. and Mrs. Irving, I can't say with certainty, but strangely both his tibia and fibula broke in two. I'm sorry to say, but I don't believe that Kyle will ever be able to play basketball again."

"Mommy, I wanna see Daddy." Gabby reached up for her mother to grab her.

Mercedes knew Gabby needed comforting too at the moment, she just wished she didn't have to pick up her ever growing four-year-old. She picked Gabby up, and then went to sit down with her in the nearest chair as she tried to digest the news the doctor had told them.

Karen was numb. She heard what the doctor said and being a sportscaster she knew what the outcome of injuries like Kyle's could possibly be, but to hear that Kyle would possibly never do what he absolutely loved again scared her. Her brain raced wondering how Kyle would react to the news.

Kyle's father rubbed his salt and pepper goatee. Frown lines etched his forehead. He squeezed his wife's shoulders as he sensed she was crying. "Come on, honey, let's have a seat." He escorted his wife to a chair and then sat beside her.

"I'll be back in a bit to let you all know when he'll be transferred to a post-op room." The surgeon nodded apologetically and walked off.

Karen stood still in the same spot. She slowly grabbed her temples trying to stop them from throbbing.

"Come on, Karen, sit down." Kyle's father gently grabbed her by her shoulders and led her to the open chair next to his wife.

Mrs. Irving reached over and grabbed Karen's hand. They squeezed each other's hands in silence.

***

"Here." Karen handed Kyle a cup of chamomile tea hoping it would soothe his mind.

"I don't want it."

"Kyle, you need to eat or at least drink something. You haven't had anything since you've come home from the hospital, and that's been three days."

Karen held on to the coffee mug as she stood over his stretched out body on the couch. "Here, drink this. I'm certain it will make you feel better."

"I said I don't want it, Karen," he mumbled.

"Okay." She took the coffee mug back to the kitchen and returned with a bowl of soup. "Okay, no tea, but would you please eat this soup? How do you expect to get better, get stronger, get back to playing ball if you aren't even eating?" Karen extended her hands with the bowl of soup towards Kyle.

His voice raised and his body stiffened. "I said I didn't want the damn tea and I don't want this damn soup either." He snatched the bowl from Karen and threw it at the wall space across the room. Pieces of corn, carrots, and string beans clung to the crevices of the brick wall as the broth slid down the wall until it formed a puddle on the floor. The bowl once containing the soup lay shattered at the base of the wall.

Karen knew that Kyle was sad and upset with the news of him never playing basketball again, but it was only so much more of his sour attitude that she would be able to take.

They didn't live together, but she practically had moved in to tend to him since the night of his freak accident on the court.

His mother and father stopped by daily trying to relieve Karen of watching after Kyle, but his somber disposition managed to run them off as well eventually.

Even Gabrielle's presence daily didn't seem to get him out of the agony he was experiencing. Not from the sustained pain in his leg, but from the news that he would never play basketball again; he would never get his championship ring.

Karen knew his anger wasn't with her, but she had no plans of being anyone's doormat ever. "Kyle, I know that you are frustrated with your leg and possibly your career ending, but you don't have to take it out on me." She rolled her eyes at him and stomped to the kitchen. She gathered what she needed to clean up the broken glass from the bowl and the remaining soup on the floor and wall.

Kyle rolled over on the couch and buried his head under a pillow.

Karen finished cleaning up. "I'll be in your bedroom if you need me, jerk!"

11

"What?" Aaron said to Melanie. "Why are you looking at me like that?"

"I don't know." Melanie blushed. *Thank God I'm dark and he can't see that my cheeks are really red.*

"Yes you do. For as opinionated as you are, you know exactly why you keep looking at me like that. Don't think that because I'm driving I haven't caught how many times you keep stealing glances at me. I know I'm fine and all, but use some tact will ya while you're staring at me." He smirked and looked straight ahead at the road.

Melanie's eyes blinked rapidly. "Whatever. I admit that you are handsome." *No, girl, he is fine. Those full lips call out to you whenever he talks, and those slanted, shaped hazel eyes against his olive skin has had you crossing your legs tight many a night you've stayed up on the phone face-timing him. Focus, Melanie.* She brought herself out of her head and back into the car with Aaron. "But that's not why I keep looking at you, I just don't…"

"You don't what? You can tell me."

"I can't. You wouldn't understand. It might come out the wrong way."

"Melanie." He looked at her the best he could while driving. "Just tell me what's on your mind."

His long, black eyelashes looked as if they tickled his eyelids as Melanie stared at him.

"Well, if you want the truth, I…" She sat up straight in her seat, but shoved her hands in between her legs trying to ground herself before she told him how she really felt. "I don't understand why I like you as much as I do."

Aaron chuckled. "What? You act like liking me is a bad thing."

"It is."

"And why is that?"

"Because I'm black and you're white."

"I thought we established that already."

"Yes, clearly anyone can see that, but it's just not right."

"Says who?" Aaron gripped the steering wheel tighter.

"A lot of people."

"We've talked about this already." Aaron sighed. "And besides, you've never pegged me as the type to do as others want you to."

"I'm not, it's just that I'm for the uplifting of my people. I love to see strong black men, black couples. I wanna be an example to younger generations of black girls to love the skin they're in and not give into the media's mass perception that we are nothing more than sex objects. How can I do that if I'm with a white man?"

Aaron slammed on the breaks. Luckily for them it was a red light and there were no cars behind him. He looked over to her. "So, you can't be who you wanna be dating me?"

"No. I can't go to a protest rallying for equality for blacks and I have a white man on my arm." Melanie poked her lips out in frustration.

"You do know the root word of equality means equal?"

Melanie crossed her arms. "Of course I know that."

"So then, you really aren't for equality if you would discriminate against me and not let me in your heart because I'm white."

Melanie stared at him. She looked up at the light. "The light is green, you should go."

"No, I'm going to sit here until I get you to see how hypocritical you're being."

"You'll never know what it's like to be me."

"You're right, I'll never know what it's like to be a woman. I'm a man." Aaron laughed.

"Whatever; you know what I mean. What it's like to be black. To feel like you have the weight of your ancestors, your race, on your shoulders."

"Who asked you to do that?"

Horns honked behind them.

"You really should go."

"Nope." He put the car in park.

"You're nuts."

"No, you are, with your archaic thinking. I'm certain it's apparent to a blind person how attracted we are to one another. How we get each other, outside of your race thinking of course, and yet you keep trying to dismiss your feelings for me because of what someone else might think of us being together. Is your hesitancy solely about the color of my skin, or is there something else to it?"

Melanie huffed and turned her head to look out the passenger window. She hadn't told Aaron yet about how her last boyfriend ended up being her brother. She was split down the middle with why she knew she couldn't be with Aaron. On one side of the coin, he was white, and on the other side, it was that he was a man and she wasn't sure if she could trust herself to pick out the right man for her; her intuition led her astray the last time.

Aaron looked over at Melanie. Her face was tight and pensive. "Melanie, you can talk to me about anything."

A squad car pulled up next to them and motioned for Aaron to let the passenger's window down. "Sir, is there a problem? You sat through a green light."

"No, sir. Everything is fine." Aaron flashed a smile at the officer.

"Okay, just make sure that you drive off when the light turns green again." The officer sped through the red light.

Aaron let Melanie's window up again.

"See, had that been me or a black man driving, the officer wouldn't have been so friendly. He would've pulled us over and pulled a gun on us. I probably would've ended up on the nine o'clock news as a tragic 'routine' stop by an officer."

The light turned green again. Aaron put the car in drive and finally pulled off. "Melanie." He reached out to grab her hand.

She reluctantly allowed his hand to intertwine with hers.

"I know the history of our country. True, I will never know what it's like to be black in America, but I do know how I feel about you. Yes, it's been such a short time since we've known each other, but you gotta be honest with yourself, there's something special between us and it becomes more potent and apparent with each passing day. We hardly sleep at night for face-timing with each other, and when we're not at our businesses, we're with each other. Again, I dare not say that I know what it's like to be black, but I wish you wouldn't let your blackness hinder what could become of us."

With a pleasant look on her face, Melanie raised an eyebrow before she said, "My blackness?"

The laugh lines on Aaron's face deepened and he cleared his throat. "Yeah, whatever it is going on in your head about you being black that's dictating to you who you should be with based on their race. For someone who clearly doesn't like being discriminated against, you're doing a great job of discriminating against me. Against what could become of us because I'm white." He said the last of his statement in a nasal nerdy like tone.

Melanie looked at his eyelashes flirting with his eyelids again. She stared at how his muscular quads filled out his jeans quite well. His right thigh muscles flexed when his foot went from pressing on the gas versus the brakes. She loved his sporty scent and how it filled the car. It seemed to be the perfect blend with her coconut oil and Shea butter mixture she was wearing. She slowly batted her eyes as if he were looking at her, although he couldn't since he was driving. "I'm trying not to let the color of your skin hinder my interest in you, but..."

"We'll leave this topic alone for now." He turned up the music in the car. The R&B artist, D'angelo's "Cruisin" filled the car with its smooth mellow sound. "Let's just enjoy the rest of this ride to the play." He pulled her hand up to his lips and slowly pecked the back of her hand.

"I love it when we're cruising together..." He sang along with D'angelo.

***

Wanting to do something special for their date and knowing that Melanie was into the arts and theater, Aaron picked a small stage play for them to see.

They walked into the theater and realized that it would be an up close and personal production since it only held twenty seats for audience members.

"Come on, let's sit up front." Aaron escorted Melanie to the first row.

He took her coat from her, put it on the back of her chair, and did the same with his.

"So, what's this play about?" Melanie looked up at him, glad that the conversation between them was no longer about race.

"I don't know. I just know that it's called 'Colors' so I figured it had something to do with painting, you know, what you love to do." He smiled and winked at her.

"Flattery will get you nowhere with me." She playfully rolled her eyes at him. Her lips curved into a cunning smile.

"Shoot, I wish it did," Aaron murmured.

"What?" Melanie sat completely erect as she stared directly at Aaron.

His ears turned red. "No, I didn't mean it like that. I just meant, I wish me giving you compliments would loosen you up more so that you won't focus on bad stuff."

"Mmm hmmm." She hummed the sound through tight lips.

"I'm serious. Being with you that way right now is not even on my mind."

Melanie looked around to see that the audience filled in.

A woman came onstage and introduced herself. "Hi, I'm Cameron Simpson. I'm so glad you all could come out tonight to see colors through my eyes. The eyes of a biracial woman growing up in a not so post-slavery society. I hope you enjoy."

The lights dimmed as she left the stage.

Melanie shot an incredulous look at Aaron.

"What? I'm sorry. I didn't know that it would be about race. I told you I thought colors meant it would be about painting."

She cocked her head at him demanding a better answer. "So you didn't read the synopsis of the play?"

"No. If I'd did that, I wouldn't have brought you here knowing that you're already so consumed with the topic. Come on, let's go." Aaron lifted up off his seat.

Melanie pushed him back down as she whispered, "No. That would be rude. I'll sit through it." She narrowed her stare in on him.

He read the look in her eyes and knew that he was in trouble. He breathed a deep sigh as the actors took the stage.

A black man stood front and center, shoulders broad and straight in what looked to be the rags slaves wore. "I fell in love with a white woman. It should've been simple, but society said otherwise."

The spotlight dimmed on him and another immediately shined on a white woman on the stage. She was a petite blonde haired woman wearing an early-1800's dress. "I never looked at the Negroes the way my daddy looked at them; neither did my mother. There was this one, John Earl. Oh, he had the deepest skin and brightest eyes I had ever seen. I loved him from the moment I met him. I taught him how to read whenever my daddy was away from the plantation." She dropped her head. "One night when my daddy was away at a bootlegging party, John Earl and I, you know, we uh…" She fidgeted with her hands. "We uh, came together in the biblical sense and my daddy caught us. He sent John Earl away that night, but a piece of him remained with me. Ten months later I had his daughter. My daddy said the only reason he let me keep her was because she could pass for white. John Earl started my lineage of mulatto children."

The spotlight dimmed on the woman and shined brightly on a woman that looked to be in her early thirties dressed in modern clothing. Her light pale skin, but thick and tightly coiled hair gave the inclination that she was biracial. Her voice boomed when she finally said, "I," she pointed to herself, "am that lineage that Mary Ann spoke about. It's 2015 and one would think that at this point in time, the color of my skin wouldn't matter at all, but sadly that's not the case." She began pacing the front of the stage. "I have always had to struggle to prove my 'blackness' to blacks and my 'whiteness' to whites. So where has that left me? I'll tell you where, without an identity!" She clapped her hands once before she put her hands on her hips. "My hair has never been straight and blond like the other white girls in my neighborhood and school." She pulled strands of her coils straight. She let them loose and they bounced back into place. "And my skin was never dark enough for the blacks." She caressed her forearms with her head hung low. "Despite my mother and father's best efforts to raise me to love *all* of me, I just never could. With the few friends that I managed to make in my adolescent years, my black friends teased me for listening to country and rock music, while my white friends just couldn't understand the rhythm and the soul of R&B and gospel.

"Oh, when I went to college, I thought things would be different. I thought people would be more open-minded, but yet again, I found out that this day and age that we live in is just as racially warped as the years of slavery and Jim Crow. There, the whites condemned me saying I got into the school because of affirmative action, while the blacks dismissed me saying that I was able to pass for white so that's how I achieved my academic accomplishments up to that point. And don't let me get started on the dating scene. I can't seem to fit in with anyone. I'm not favored by the average black guy because I don't have the biggest and roundest butt." She turned to the side to reveal her flat butt. "And the white guys never seem to stick around too long because they can't run their fingers through my hair while we're swimming without getting them stuck in it. But this is 2015, right? Yeah, the year is 2015, but the average mind is stuck in the past, the past of condemning and judging people because of the color of their skin. Colors. When will it end?"

"Colors." Voices onstage shouted out.

"Why can't we focus more on the colors in nature and stay in awe of them instead of despicable awe of skin colors?"

"Colors."

"When will we not let the color of a person's skin, eyes, or hair determine their worth?"

"Colors."

"I'm so sick of the color of my skin, your skin, your skin," she pointed towards audience members, "determining how we treat each other."

"Colors."

"I just wish we all were color blind."

The lights onstage faded completely out. The entire room was dark.

The audience waited before they began to clap.

The lights came on in the room and the playwright came back to the stage. "Well ladies and gentleman, I hope you've enjoyed thus far. We'll take a fifteen minute intermission and then the play will resume."

The audience began filing out the room.

Melanie turned to look at Aaron.

He refused to look at her.

"Really?" she said.

"What?" He smirked.

"You know what. That's why you won't look at me. I can't believe you brought me here to see this and this is the very problem I have with us." She grabbed her coat from the back of the chair.

He jumped up to help her put it on, but she pulled away from him and walked off.

"I'm sorry," he repeated as he rushed to keep up with her.

She made it to the car before he did. She stood at the passenger's side door tapping her foot with her arms folded across her chest.

He opened the door for her and closed it once she was fully in her seat. He rushed around to the driver's side door and jumped in the car. "I guess you're really mad, hunh? You didn't reach over to open my door like you normally do."

She remained silent.

"Melanie, I told you I didn't know what the play would be about. But you have to admit, she brought up some good points."

Melanie turned to face him. Her harsh stare at him demanded the answer to his own question.

"Like why do we focus on the color of someone's skin in 2015? And I'm certain she would have said a whole lot more in my favor had we stayed for the rest." He turned the volume down on the car speakers.

"So you're just going to ignore the story of her life? How she struggled to fit in?"

"No, I got that part, but that's the problem with trying to fit in when we're born to stand out."

"Oh don't give me that rhetoric."

Aaron shook his head emphatically and laughed.

"What is so funny?" Her nostrils flared.

"You're so cute when you pout. Beautiful when you smile and cute when you pout."

Melanie looked towards the window trying to hide the smile forming on her lips. She wanted to be mad at him, get her point across, but the fluttering of his eyelashes against his eyelids and the way he talked to her made her blush and forget why she even had a problem with the two of them being together. She finally straightened her face and turned back towards him. "Who would willingly bring a child into the world to have to face those problems, the problems she faced?"

He dropped some of the humor in his voice before speaking. "No matter what color, gender, socio-economic background a person has, they will face some difficulties in life. The beliefs instilled in them and the support system around them is what will make the difference for them when they do encounter said problems."

"Yeah, but clearly the problems biracial kids and interracial couples face could be avoided." Melanie huffed.

"How? By the couple not following their hearts and being with who they want to be with?"

"Yup." Melanie pouted and folded her arms over her chest again.

"There you go being cute again." He stared at her waiting for her to break a smile.

Her face remained stoic.

He slowly reached out and touched her side and then tickled her.

Her giggling filled the car.

"See all I want to do is to make you smile, make you happy."

You do? Me too! I just wish you were black doing all of that.

***

Aaron plopped down on his couch smiling. He loved spending time with Melanie, but he wished that she would let go of the race issue with them. He firmly believed that love had no boundaries.

His phone rang.

"Hello," Aaron said into his phone.

"What up, Aaron?" Damon, Aaron's best friend, asked.

"Nothing, man. I just got back from my date with Melanie."

"Oh." Damon snarled. "So how's it going with her?"

"Great. I really like her and I can tell she likes me. It's just gonna take her a little more time than I thought to warm up to the idea of us being together."

Damon smiled. "Well, don't rush it, man. If it's meant to be, it will be."

"Yeah, I know that, but I really do think that we're meant to be together. She has to get over the color of my skin." Aaron shook his head.

"Hunh?"

"Yeah, she feels like people aren't still as accepting of interracial couples as they should be so she doesn't wanna be a 'sell-out' to her people. Crazy, right?"

Damon was silent.

Aaron sat up on the couch. "I said that's crazy, right man?"

"I mean, I can understand where she's coming from. It's one thing when you have an interracial friendship, but a romantic interracial relationship rubs people the wrong way sometimes."

Aaron stood up and said louder into the phone, "So what are you saying D, you one of those people?"

"Naw A, not me. But you've been around black folks long enough to know that everybody doesn't think that you genuinely are the way you are. Some of them think you frontin' with the way you can code switch depending on the crowd. You know, using slang with the fellas, but all proper with your English when it comes to handling business. I don't, but there are a lot of people that do."

Aaron relaxed his tensed jaw muscles and sat back down. "Well, that's good to know that you don't think like that."

"Never, A. We go back strong. I'm down for whatever with you," Damon said in a flat voice. "But you're just spoiled, man."

Aaron guffawed. "What? How am I spoiled?"

Damon slammed his balled up fist down on the countertop in his kitchen. "Because, you've always gotten whatever black woman you went after, but now you've met a sista that ain't so quick to win over like the others. She might not be the one."

"You keep saying that, but I know she is."

"Okay, so what really makes her the one?" Damon's jaws tightened.

"We love the same music, we're both entrepreneurs and passionate about what we do."

"Speaking of," Damon interrupted Aaron, "what does she do?"

"She's an artist and she owns her own art gallery called…"

Damon smiled and briefly tuned out what Aaron was saying as he slowly nodded his head in admiration of Melanie's profession.

"You say an art gallery? Where at?"

"Yeah, over on Clark Street."

"Say the name of it again." Damon grabbed a pen from his junk drawer so that he could write down the name of her gallery.

"Man, open up your ears. I said it's called Perspective."

Damon laughed. "Okay, I got it."

"Good."

"So are you gonna put her on a timeline to come around to you?"

"Naw, man, she's worth the wait. I'll just keep being me and treating her the way she deserves to be treated, and I'm certain that she'll come around soon enough."

"You always were cocky when it came to women." Damon grimaced.

"Naw, it ain't even like that. I'm just confident enough to go after whoever or whatever I want. Shoot, I got that from you." Aaron laughed.

"Yeah, I hear ya, because I'm definitely going after what I want this time around." Damon smiled.

"Well, alright man, let me go and get some rest. I've got to be at the store all day tomorrow."

"Cool. Well, I'll holla at you soon. And keep me updated about your progress with what's her name?"

"Her name is Melanie." Aaron smiled.

"Okay, Melanie." Damon smiled. "And you only told me two things y'all have in common. The next time we talk, you have to tell me more about her."

"Bet," Aaron said.

"Aiight," Damon said.

"Aiight, bye."

"Mel-la-nie. Melanie. Damon and Melanie. That sounds better than Melanie and Aaron. Yeah, Damon and Melanie." Damon walked to his living room smiling. He sat down on his couch to look her up on social media.

12

Marie stood in the mirror near her front door smoothing out her sweater and patting her soft curls into place. She leaned in closer to the mirror and pulled back the corners of her eyes trying to will away the creases that had formed into noticeable wrinkles over the years.

She shook her head knowing that time wasn't the only culprit in the way she had aged over the years, but moreso the turmoil and agony of her rape. That and giving her son up for adoption. She smiled the more she looked at herself realizing she still didn't look as bad as she could have given her mental state over the years.

She ran her tongue over her straight, white teeth making sure nothing was hiding in the crevices.

The doorbell rang.

She took a deep breath and stepped over into the front of the door. She smoothed out her hair and sweater one more time. She took another deep breath and slowly opened the door.

On the other side of it stood her ex-husband, Melanie's father, Howard Daniels.

He was even more handsome than she remembered.

Well, I see he kept himself up. "Come in." She opened the door fully and he walked in.

It had been a long time since they had last seen each other and Marie didn't quite know how to greet him. *Should I hug him? Shake his hand? Why is he making me so nervous right now? I know this man. Or do I?* She laughed out loud at herself.

Howard smiled. "Since you don't know what to do, I'll help you." He grabbed both of her hands into his and pulled her into his embrace.

Marie's eyes closed as her arms rested on his broad shoulders and wrapped around his neck. *He must workout as strong as he is.*

Howard took a deep breath inhaling the scent of her hair. He always loved the way she smelled. It was tropical sweet, but not too fruity. Similar to a coconut, Howard knew her hard and withdrawn shell covered up the sweet, soft, and caring woman she was on the inside. Him looking past her aloof exterior is what made him fall for her when they were younger. He saw right to the core of her—a beautiful heart, apparently wounded, but beautiful nonetheless. He thought he could love her past her pain and out of her despair but five years into their lopsided marriage and a precious baby girl later, she never really opened up to him. He ended their marriage thinking that maybe his constant watch of her and catering to her was actually hindering the breakthrough she seemingly needed.

They finally pulled apart from one another, but he didn't let go of her hands. He stared at her for a moment in silence taking in the beautiful wrinkles on her face.

She stared back at him, soaking up how handsome he was and how his salt and pepper goatee framed his square jawbones. His chocolate skin appeared to be smoother than what it was when they were younger. She couldn't help herself, she reached out and caressed his cheek. Realizing that she had actually touched his face, she tried to pull her hand away but he captured hers in his and held it near his face before kissing her hand.

She smiled, blushing.

He stared into her. The glow he saw in her eyes excited him. He could finally see the woman he fell in love with so many years ago had awakened.

"Come." She broke the trance he held her in and led him into the kitchen with one hand.

He gladly followed behind her.

"Have a seat." Marie pointed to the chair she wanted him to sit in.

Howard took his coat off and hung it on the back of the chair.

Marie was busy at the island gathering food to take to the table for them to eat.

Howard smiled staring at her.

She walked back and forth from the countertop with her hands full of small platters of food and placed them on the table.

"Shall we?" She waved her hand over the food letting him know that he could dig in when he wanted to.

He sat at the end of the table and Marie sat on a side of the table to the left of him.

He reached out to grab her hand and she placed hers in his.

"Bow your head and let's pray," he instructed.

Marie obliged. She smiled as she felt the gentle tightening of his grip on her hand.

"Thank you, God, for this food we're about to receive. We ask that it be nourishment to our bodies and sustain us until we eat again."

Marie looked up prepared to say amen thinking that Howard was done, but he looked into her eyes as he continued to pray.

"And Lord, thank You for this hand I now hold. Thank You that she is free in You. Thank You for reconnecting us and we pray that moving forward, Your will will be done in our lives. In Jesus' name."

Together they said amen.

They stared into each other's eyes a little longer before Marie broke their trance and began placing food on his plate.

"Salad?" Marie asked.

"Yes." He smiled at her.

"Soup?"

"Yes."

"Bread?"

"Yup."

"So, how have you been? I heard about your wife. I'm sorry for you loss," Marie said, cutting her lettuce. She placed her utensils at the side of her plate and patted his hand waiting for his response.

"Thank you. I've been good. We were only married for five years, but it was five great years." Howard sat back in his seat.

"I'm sorry, I didn't mean to bring her up and make you sad. It's just that I haven't seen you in ages. I want to know how you've been."

"It's okay. And yes, it's been way too long since we've last seen each other. What, ten years?"

"Yup. Melanie's college graduation, right?"

"Yup, and before that, it had been since her high school graduation…" Howard pulled his chair from the table and brought it closer to Marie. He searched her eyes trying to gauge if she was really ready to open up to him. When he saw a light in them he hadn't seen there when they were married, he figured it was okay to continue on. "What happened to you? What happened to us?"

"Well, I see you didn't waste any time getting straight to the point." Marie pushed her chair back and tried to get up from her seat, but Howard managed to pull her chair closer to him caging her in with his arms as he firmly held on to the lower sides of the chair.

Marie had no choice but to sit back down.

"I let you run away from me, from whatever was haunting you when we were married, but I won't let you do that now."

Marie's eyes widened. She chuckled. "So you're just gonna hold me hostage until I fess up?"

"If that's what it'll take."

"What happened to that gentle man I was married to? The one who let me wallow without any interference."

"He's long gone." Howard stared at her. Her smooth, almond colored skin was still beautiful to him. She no longer wore her hair long and straight as she had when they were married. It was now cut above her shoulders. Her curls were big and tousled. He loved the style on her. He had to stop admiring her beauty and continue their conversation. "Maybe if I hadn't been so docile then, maybe you'd told me what was going on with you; maybe you wouldn't have wallowed for so long."

Tears seeped from Marie's eyes. She cleared her throat before speaking. "So do you know what happened to me?" She looked into his eyes searching for the answer.

"No."

"Why not? I know that you and Mel are close. I figured she would've told you by now."

"She wanted to, but we both agreed that it would be better if *you* told me."

Marie pouted. "I wish she would've told you. Then I wouldn't have to now."

The raspiness in her voice always did something to him. He always thought it was one of the many attributes of her that made her so beautiful.

"Are you ready to talk, to tell me about it now?"

She took a deep breath. "Can you give me a moment to gather myself first?"

"Sure." He said.

She chuckled. "Will you let me get up?"

He smiled. "Yes, but I won't let you run away from me anymore." He backed his seat up allowing her room enough to get up from hers.

She walked over to the sink and let the water run before she washed her hands. She didn't towel dry her hands, rather she dabbed at her face with her wet hands.

Howard came up behind her and handed her a dry dish towel.

"Thanks." She took it from him and dried her hands.

He leaned back against the island with his hands folded at his chest.

She stared at him grinding his teeth and how the motion made his strong jawline flex.

"Why are you staring at me like that?" Howard's eyebrows wrinkled in wonder.

Marie blushed. "I hate to admit this outloud, but you're more handsome than I remembered." She dropped her head.

"Well, that's because you never paid much attention to me while we were together. It's a wonder how we even made Melanie."

She pulled her hands up to her face and mumbled through her hands. "I'm sorry. I wasn't a good wife to you. I never really was intimate with you. Looking back, it's a miracle how I even had the wherewithall to date you, let alone marry you."

He walked over to Marie and carefully pulled her hands from her face. "You don't have to be. Come on, let's go into the living room and talk." Howard gripped her smooth and slender hand and gently pulled her into the living room and helped her to sit on the couch. He sat next to her as they sat in silence forgetting about the uneaten food they left in the kitchen.

Marie leaned her head on Howard's shoulder and instinctively, he wrapped his arm around her shoulder allowing her to nestle under his arm.

Silence remained between them for a while before Marie heaved a deep breath and said, "Howard, I was raped." She wiped her nose with the sleeve of her sweater.

He reached over his balding head and grabbed tissue from the tissue box sitting on the table behind the couch and handed some to Marie.

She cleaned her nose as she continued to lean on him. "Did you hear me? I was raped."

"I heard you."

She lifted up from him. "So that doesn't shock you? Turn you off?"

"No."

She scooted away from him on the couch. "Well, it shocked me. It turned me off from myself."

"I take it back, I am shocked."

"See I knew it." She turned her head from him.

He edged over closer to her. "I'm shocked that you never told me about it."

She gazed at him trying to understand what he was saying.

"It happened before we met?"

"Yes." She dropped her head in shame.

"So why didn't you tell me? I wouldn't have judged you."

"You say that, but you don't know what it's like."
She stood up and paced the floor. "I went through so
many emotions after I was raped. I blamed myself
for letting it happen. I hated him for doing it to me.
And then I had that beautiful baby boy as a reminder
of it all. You didn't know that, did you? You didn't
know I had a child before Melanie, did you?"

Howard stared at Marie as she paced the floor
holding herself.

"No, I didn't know you had a child."

With bloodshot eyes, she pointed at him. "I bet if
you did you wouldn't have wanted me."

Howard stood up and walked over to Marie. He
caressed her face creased with worry lines and she
laid her head on his hand and cried some more
before he pulled her into an embrace.

With his hug, he tried to pour out all of the love
he had for her. He hoped the strength in his arms and
in his stature would calm whatever worries and
soothe any doubts she had about herself, about him.

She continued to weep in his arms. "I'm sorry,
Howard. I'm sorry I didn't love you the way you
deserved to be loved. I'm sorry I pushed you away."

He held onto her tightly as he navigated their way
back to the couch.

She leaned in closely to him until her sobs
subsided.

He handed her more tissues and she wiped her
broad nose.

He lifted her chin until their eyes met. "I wish you
would've trusted me back then with all of this."

"I just couldn't. I knew you loved me, but I couldn't see past my pain." Her eyebrows knitted together as she shook her head staring at him. "Why did you want me anyway?"

"Because I saw past your pain." He smiled at her. "I saw your heart of gold despite how withdrawn you were from me and the world."

"Well, if you loved me so, why did you leave me then?" Marie pouted.

He held onto her chin. "I didn't want to, but you pushed me away so much, so far, that I figured maybe if I weren't around and doing everything for you, for Melanie, you might come out of your stupor."

"Well, it didn't work." She managed to pout and smirk almost at the same time.

"Not then, but I see that you're getting past it now."

"I'm trying to." She fiddled with her fingers.

"I'm here to help you now, if you'll let me." Howard stared into Marie's eyes as he leaned in closer to her. With his lips millimeters from hers and feeling the heat of her breath on his skin, he searched her eyes for an indication that she wanted him to stop. When he didn't see any hesitation in them, he placed his lips on hers. She never kissed him back when they were married, but she parted her lips allowing his tongue to mingle with hers.

She kissed him like she never had kissed him before, with her heart.

13

Although Melanie still had a major issue with Aaron being white, she couldn't seem to get enough of him.

He pulled on a part of her heart that she didn't even know existed. That scared her because she thought what she and Andrew had was special and real, but she saw how that turned out. Still, she wasn't ready to be so willing to freely give her love to Aaron only to find out that the difference between their races was too much for her to handle.

Despite her reservations, she kept on talking to him as much as she could and going out on dates with him.

She stood in the mirror readying herself for their date that night. She frowned thinking on how a year ago, Karen would have stormed into her bathroom while she was prepping to go out, but now that Karen was with Kyle, she and Karen had been spending less and less time together. She missed her friend.

As she played with her curls trying to place her hair the exact way she wanted it, she smiled thinking about how she held her breath the first time Aaron had coyly played in her hair as she sat in the passenger seat of his car. She was taken aback by his gesture. She remembered readying herself to explain why his fingers would never make it through the ends of her strands, but he never allowed his fingers to leave her scalp as he gently massaged it. It felt so good to her at the time that she dare not bring it up or the fact that if they ever went swimming together, water would never cascade down long, straight tresses of hers like the swimsuit models, but rather hers would look like a fluffy brillo pad after her first dip in the water.

He amazed her sometimes at how her cultural norms didn't shock him, like her putting sugar in her grits when they went to breakfast one morning. In fact, he loaded more sugar in his grits than she did in hers. She smiled thinking about how her eyes bulged as she watched him do it. He told her not to judge him and that although he was into his health, sugar in his grits was something he wasn't willing to give up.

She applied her lipstick and giggled thinking about how the first time she was at his house, she helped herself to get a drink because he was on the phone with an employee at his shoe store. She looked in the refrigerator to find that he had made three jugs of different flavors of Kool-Aid. She poured a little of each to see how they tasted, but immediately had to spit each of them out because they were too sweet for her liking. When she teased him about it, he reminded her that he grew up around blacks and sweet Kool-Aid was the only way to go. He winked at her and told her he had a sweet tooth.

She puckered her lips making sure her lipstick was evenly applied before she turned to go in her closet to pick something out to wear.

After their date at the play, she insisted that she plan their dates from that point on, but he told her to trust him. The next one would be better.

It was something in his voice. The way he told her to trust him made her yield to his request.

The whereabouts of their date would be a surprise to her, so she didn't know how to dress. With not much to go off of, she decided on a plum colored sweater dress with a cowl neckline. She reasoned she would be warm if they went somewhere with the air conditioner on, even though the Chicago winter was in full effect. On the other hand, if they went somewhere that was warm, she could push up her sleeves and the draping neckline on her sweater-dress would provide intermittent pockets of air to her upper body.

She was dressed and waiting downstairs in the lobby of her building since Aaron had called her to say that he would be pulling up soon.

"Ms. Daniels, you sure do look pretty tonight." Lonnie, the doorman and concierge for the building, looked up from his surveillance screen at Melanie.

"Thanks, Mr. Lonnie. You look handsome as always." Melanie smiled as she walked over to his desk.

"Oh, you and Ms. Roberts are so sweet to me, and my wife loves y'all for it."

"How is she?" Melanie cupped her chin as she leaned on the countertop with her elbows.

"She's great. She worries about me still working here at my age, but I tell her I'm fine. The tenants here, like yourself, are great. So my day runs smoothly for the most part."

"Your age?" Melanie stood up straight and put her hands on her hip. "Mr. Lonnie, you can't be a day over fifty, so why would she worry about you still working at *your* age?"

He grinned. "Aren't you the sweetest. Melanie, I made seventy at the beginning of this year, and with the Lord willing, I'll be making seventy-one at the beginning of the new year."

"No." Melanie's mouth dropped open. She was honestly shocked. She leaned in closer to him. "You're kidding me, right?"

He smiled. "No, I'm not."

"You look great at your age."

"Thanks."

"How do you still look so young? You barely have any wrinkles. Your skin is glowing and you look like you're in good shape. You never walk around dragging your feet. I've never seen you with glasses on. And I'm guessing those are still your real teeth." Melanie giggled. "Come on, you can tell me, do you dye your hair? There is barely any gray up there."

"Nope, I don't dye it. And these are my real teeth." Lonnie chomped the air. "It's been the good

Lord that has kept me like this. And you know black don't crack." He winked at her while rubbing his mocha colored cheek.

Melanie exchanged a knowing look with him.

"Well, you know it's true, plus my wife and I work out at least four days a week together."

"That is so adorable."

"If you don't mind me saying, but for a while there I was afraid of how fast you were aging."

Melanie's eyebrows squished together in wonder.

"It seems like you had gotten depressed there for a while after Ms. Roberts wedding."

Melanie squinted her eyes at him.

He chuckled a little. "Yeah, I know she didn't get married, but still, after that day, you seemed so deflated. Lost some weight. You just weren't your vibrant self for a minute, but I see you've gotten the pep back in your step."

Melanie smiled.

"Does it have something to do with that young man that's been picking you up lately?"

Melanie smiled and slowly nodded her head, blushing.

"Well, good then. We shouldn't seek for happiness in others, but when we find someone in life who helps to make us happy, we should hold on to that person."

Melanie stood quiet soaking in all that Lonnie was saying.

"Well, it looks like a part of your happiness is here." He pointed to Aaron walking through the large glass front doors.

Aaron walked over to Melanie and kissed her on her cheek. "Hello, beautiful. You ready?" He stared at her with such admiration.

"Yes, but let me introduce you to Mr. Lonnie first."

Aaron nodded.

"Aaron, this is Mr. Lonnie, Mr. Lonnie, this is Aaron." Melanie looked between the two of them.

Aaron extended his hand first. Lonnie accepted and the two equally gripped one another's hands.

"Firm handshake, young man. And you looked me in my eyes when you shook my hand. I like that. That speaks of what kind of man you are." He smiled and nodded.

"Yes, sir. I was raised to do no less."

"And I'm glad about that. Now you two enjoy yourselves tonight and take good care of my little friend here. Good evening." Lonnie nodded his head at Aaron and Melanie.

Aaron smiled. "Enjoy the rest of your evening, sir, and again, sir, I was raised to do no less than to take good care of her."

Aaron extended his elbow to Melanie. "Shall we?"

"We shall." She smiled at him and locked her elbow with his as they walked out of the building arm and arm.

***

"Where are you taking me?" Melanie asked for the umpteenth time as Aaron opened her car door.

"Woman, just trust me."

"Um, I'm trying, but after that play you chose, I don't know if I should."

Aaron laughed as he playfully nudged her. "Will you let that go already? I did my research on this place and I'm certain you will enjoy it." He laced his fingers with hers as they walked down the street.

She smiled. It was the little things he did that made her like him more and more. Like making her walk on the inside of the sidewalk instead of him being nonchalant and allowing her to walk on the sidewalk near the curb.

She took pleasure in the way he grabbed her hand without asking. She liked his balance of being courteous of what she wanted and at the same time doing little things to show her he was a man that could take charge. That's why despite wanting to fight him on picking the place for their date that night, she decided to see if she could really trust him to handle things. Without trust, there really was no future for them.

The strong artic-like winds whipped past them and at times, it seemed to whip through them. She had on a floor length down coat and gloves, but he sensed her shivering as she was no match for the Windy City's cold front, so he pulled her closer to him as they walked trying to warm her up.

"I'm sorry we couldn't park closer. You see I circled the block a few times but couldn't find a place to park. I didn't want us to be late for what I have planned trying to find a parking space."

"It's okay. You know I grew up in Chicago, so I know all about the lack of parking up north. Thanks though. Are we there yet?" Melanie looked over to Aaron as her teeth were chattering.

"Man, you're cute when you're cold." He smiled bright. "And yes, we're here."

Melanie looked through the window of the storefront to see that it was a sip and paint location. She looked back at him. "Thank you."

"My pleasure." He smiled and walked ahead of her a few feet to hold the door open for her.

She walked through the doors; he followed closely behind her and they were both greeted by the host. "Welcome. What are your names?"

"My name is Aaron Oliver and this is the beautiful and amazing Melanie Daniels."

The host looked down at her clipboard searching for their names.

"Okay, good. You're all checked in. I see this is your first time here Mr. Oliver, but Ms. Daniels you've been to one of our other locations before, I see."

"Yes." Melanie smiled at her.

Aaron raised his eyebrows. He whispered in her ear. "I hope only with Karen and not on a date with another man." His eyebrows furrowed.

She laughed looking at him. "Oh, you're so cute when you're being nosey with a little hint of jealousy."

"Your easels are set up over here." The host walked them to where they would be seated.

"Someone will be with you in a moment to take your wine order."

"Okay. Thank you," Aaron said.

"Thanks," Melanie said.

"You're more than welcome." The host walked off, but stopped in her tracks and slowly pivoted in a 180 degree circle until she faced Melanie again. With a puzzled look on her face she tapped Melanie on her shoulder.

Melanie turned to her smiling. "Yes?"

"I'm sorry to bother you, but you wouldn't happen to be thee Melanie Daniels? Owner of Perspective? One of the best Chicago artist, artist of our time for that matter?"

Melanie blushed, but again, her chocolate skin hid her rosy cheeks. "Yes and thank you." Melanie smiled.

The host extended her hand to shake Melanie's.

Melanie accepted the hosts hand while keeping her laughter at bay seeing as though the host had somehow turned into a fanatic admirer of hers.

"I'm sorry I can't stop shaking your hand, but your work is what made me love art so much! I visit your gallery all of the time. You never have enough of your pieces out on display. Oh how I wish that you would put your work out for everyone to see like when you first started." The more she talked the more high-pitched her voice became. "Did I say I love your work? Did I even tell you my name?" She didn't wait for Melanie to answer. "I'm sorry for being so rude, my name is Tonya."

"Nice to meet you, Tonya." Melanie smiled.

Tonya continued on her rant with her eyes wide with excitement. "I knew you looked familiar when you came in, but I just knew thee Melanie Daniels wouldn't come to a simple paint shop like ours with the talent you have. Oh my goodness, do you have some new pieces? I would love to stop by and see them sometime if you'll let me." She covered her face in shame. "Oh my goodness, my piece is the one you all will be mimicking tonight. I'm so embarrassed for you to see it. I know it pales in comparison to what you would do with the subject matter."

Melanie placed her hands on the host's shoulders. She smiled as she said, "Calm down, it's okay. I know your piece will be great."

"Thank you." Tonya worked to catch her breath.

"Can we keep your piece here? Please."

"Sure, if that's fine with my date." Melanie looked to Aaron for assurance.

He nodded his head in amazement.

"Yes." The host balled her fist and pumped it in the air in a triumphant motion. "Do you like red or white wine? Just let me know. I'll have my server pull you all a bottle from our special collection."

"That won't be necessary," Melanie said.

"No, it would be my pleasure." She exhaled a deep breath. "I'm sorry for losing my composure with you and sounding like a groupie, but your work really inspires me. I'm sorry I have to rush off, but there are others waiting at the door."

"No problem. Go handle your business," Melanie said.

Tonya smiled and walked back to the front of the shop.

"Wow." Aaron's eyes were wide and his mouth still hung open.

"What?" Melanie allowed Aaron to help her take her coat off.

"I didn't know you had it like that."

Melanie laughed.

"I mean, I've seen your work at the gallery. It is amazing, but I didn't know you had a following like her. She was crazy over you."

"I've never gotten a response like that before, but when I first introduced my paintings to the world, I sold a lot of them for lofty prices which allowed me to invest my money into my gallery and some other things to make money while I sleep." Melanie smiled. "But it became about more than making money from my paintings, I wanted to help other artists reach their full potential and get maximum exposure. That translated into me teaching art classes at the time."

Aaron nodded his head smiling at Melanie. He handed their coats to an employee who stood waiting to take them. "Okay, so why don't you still teach art classes if that's your desire?"

They sat on their stools.

"I did for a few years, but there's a bureaucracy to teaching that I don't like. And there were some amazing artists that never set foot in a classroom. I wanted to be around those kind of artists so I opened up my gallery for classes for a while, but then I just wanted to work on helping to expose artist's work."

"Okay, but when you speak about art, you speak with such passion, I think you should teach a few classes here and there again."

Melanie pursed her lips. "Mmmph. Maybe I will, but enough about me. I bet you have 'fans' coming in your store all of the time," Melanie teased, jabbing him in the side with her elbow.

"I sell shoes, I don't make them." Aaron laughed.

"True."

"Well, Ms. Artiste, please try not to show me up tonight."

"I'll try not to. Hey, to even the playing field, how about I paint with my right hand."

"Hunh?" Aaron's eyebrows furrowed.

"I'm left-handed, so painting with my right hand should be challenging for me." Melanie smiled.

"Okay, let's shake on it."

They shook hands, but held onto each other's hand noting yet again, the magnetic chemistry they had as they stared into each other eyes.

Melanie was enjoying Aaron with no thought of the color of his skin until a group of women sat down near her.

"Girl, he must have money."

"You know it. That's the only reason why she's probably with him. Because you know he ain't packing like a brotha, if you know what I mean. Okay!" The caramel colored lady high-fived the first woman who spoke.

Another woman in her group shook her head at the first two hagglers before speaking. "I can't take you two anywhere without y'all making a scene and being ignorant. Mind your business and leave the woman alone. Y'all don't know what she's capable of doing."

"Please!" The first woman said. "I wish she would step to me because of what I'm saying. This is America. I know my rights. The first amendment guarantees me freedom of speech." She smacked her lips at her reasonable friend.

"Right. Plus, ain't no real sista gone be with a white man. A real sista would be with a brotha. One who would ride or die for her. This one here, trying to look down with her natural hair, is probably one of those self-hating pushover types." She pointed to Melanie.

Remembering how she responded to the manager at the soul food restaurant, and clearly seeing the fire in Melanie's eyes as they listened to the women speaking about her, Aaron held a firm grip on Melanie's arm keeping her on her stool for as long as he could, but she broke free of him and turned around to be face to face with the women who spoke so negatively of her.

"Yes, you have the freedom of speech, but that freedom doesn't keep you from the consequences of this self-aware black woman from putting her long foot up your ass if you don't chill with your ignorant comments."

The woman who first made rude comments curled her lips and wrinkled her nose as she walked in front of Melanie. "Who you talking to?" Her voice raised louder than anyone else in the room.

All eyes were now on Melanie and her hagglers.

"I'm talking to y'all!" She pointed to the other woman. "You have the nerve to say I'm the 'self-hating' type, but I'm not the one up in here with blonde hair glued to my head, in a ridiculous bird-like style might I add, with green contacts. Because I do love myself, the skin I'm in, my blackness, I'm not trying to hide it with hideous and unmatchable cosmetics. I mean really. You're talking about me not loving myself, but you and I are the same color and yet you have on foundation that's three shades lighter than what you are. Really, who's fooling who?"

"Look trick—" the woman in Melanie's face raised her hand to Melanie, but her sensible friend pulled her back as Tonya walked over to them.

"Melanie, is there a problem here?" Tonya stood in between Melanie and the other two ladies who were pretending like they were struggling to get to Melanie, although their friend really didn't have a hold of them.

"Yes, Tonya, there is a problem. These two women have been disrespectful to me and my date since they came over here. They thought I was a punk, and I normally try to avoid altercations, but I couldn't let it slide with what they were saying, racist and defaming comments."

Tonya turned to the women. "Ladies, racism and confrontations are not allowed in my establishment. I'm going to have to ask you all to leave please."

The two boisterous women didn't budge, however their responsible friend grabbed her coat from the guy standing near them.

The two ratchet ones stood in place with their hands on their sides. The first one to initiate talk of Melanie said, "I'm waiting on you to put her out, too! She was just as aloud as we were."

Tonya remained silent as she stared at the demanding woman.

The woman folded her arms at her chest and bucked her head at Tonya. "I'm not leaving until she leaves."

"Ricky," Tonya yelled out.

A burly, six foot three man appeared from the back room.

"Can you escort these ladies out for me please, sweety?"

"Yes, dear. Let's go, ladies." Tonya's husband, the burly man, pointed towards the door.

"I know you bet not put yo' hands on me." The other woman snarled as she snatched her purse from the table.

The loudest woman stopped in her tracks at the door. "Hold up. I'll leave, but since we paid, you need to run me a refund before I get out of here."

Tonya walked towards the front door. "No, ma'am. When you signed up for this class, you signed an electronic agreement with the knowledge that you would only be refunded your payment if the studio canceled the event, but no refunds for your inability to show up or any misconduct on your part."

"Hold up! Hold up! So, what you saying is, I can't stay and paint and sip wine, but I can't get my money back either?" She cocked her head to the side waiting for Tonya to respond.

"Exactly. Please escort them out, Ricky."

"Ladies, please leave now." The bass and sternness of Ricky's voice let the ladies know that it was best that they not try his patience.

Aaron stood holding Melanie's wrist unsure if she would try to chase after the women.

"That's okay. We'll leave now, but I better not catch that nappy headed heffa..." The woman continued to talk as she walked down the street to her car.

Tonya walked back over to where Melanie and Aaron stood.

Aaron's face was red.

Tonya grabbed Melanie's available hand and held it firmly. She looked up at Melanie. "Oh my God, Melanie. I am so sorry that you had to endure that. I mean that was ridiculous. I can't believe the nerve of some people. How dare they—"

"Tonya, it's okay." Melanie pulled her hand from Tonya's grip. "It wasn't your fault."

Tonya put her hand up to her chest and breathed a sigh of relief. "Thank God you're not mad at me. I totally understand if you want to leave right now after all of that. I would definitely reimburse you two, but I really hope you will stay and try to enjoy what's left of the night."

Melanie stood silent and rubbed the back of her neck. She was over the night and wanted to go home. "I appreciate your courtesy towards me and my date, and yeah, I think it's best if I leave now."

Tonya frowned. "I understand." She walked ahead of them to the front desk.

The young man who took coats from guests earlier reappeared with Aaron and Melanie's coats. Aaron assisted Melanie in putting her coat on while Tonya retrieved cash from the register.

"Here." She handed Melanie eighty dollars.

Melanie gave Tonya a half smile. "Tonya, it's okay. Please keep the money."

"No, I feel so bad about what happened. I want to refund you for tonight plus offer you and your date a complimentary session." Tonya smiled.

Melanie looked Aaron up and down then rolled her eyes in frustration.

"Tonya," Melanie pushed the money back towards her, "keep the money, please. And thanks, but I won't be needing that complimentary session either." She turned and walked out the door without allowing Aaron to open it for her. Although he tried to be chivalrous as they were walking out, she was too fast in grabbing the door and letting herself out.

Aaron caught his stride up with Melanie's and tried to grab her hand, but she jerked it away from him.

The short, frequent breaths he saw steaming from her nostrils let him know that she was mad. "Melanie? Melanie, would you talk to me, please?"

Melanie ignored him and kept walking.

Aaron started the car using the remote starter. If the night would have went how he planned, he would have left her inside the venue until he went and got his car and it was warm.

They were now close enough to the car for Aaron to pop the lock. Melanie heard the clicks and rushed to let herself in and close the door before Aaron had the chance to do anything for her.

Aaron stood at her door staring at her shivering in the car.

He realized his fingers were numb from the cold so he made his way over to the driver's side and got in. He adjusted the heat settings. He blew into his hands as he looked at her. "Melanie. That wasn't my fault. I know you're not blaming me for that too, are you?"

She refused to look in his direction.

"Melanie?"

"Can you just please take me home?"

He pulled out of the parking spot and took off.

She stared at the displays of one storefront after another as they rode down the street. Each one showcasing a vintage clothing or antiques. She mumbled her thoughts out loud, "That's the problem now, everyone's thinking is so vintage."

"Hunh?" Aaron looked over at Melanie staring out of the window. "What did you say?"

"Nothing," she mumbled and angled her body completely away from him.

Aaron pulled over and parked in the first open spot he saw on the street.

"What are you doing? This is not my building."

"I know, but I'm not moving this car again until you talk to me." Aaron turned his body fully towards her.

"Well, I hope you have enough gas in here then to keep the car on, because it will be sitting here for forever. I'm tired of talking about the same thing over and over. Besides, us talking about it won't change anything."

"What won't change?"

"Me being black and you being white." Melanie turned to face Aaron. Her eyes were watery and her voice held frustration. "The way people look at us, the ignorant comments they make. Every time we've gone out, we've had to deal with some form of racism. Look how long it took us to find a breakfast spot where the employees and customers seemed to be cool with us being there with one another. I don't wanna live like this, especially not with the other stuff going on in my life."

Aaron reached for Melanie's hand. She tried to pull it from him, but the warm look in his eyes and the firm yet gentle way he gripped her hand comforted her and she relaxed somewhat with him.

"Melanie, you hint at what else is going on in your life, but you haven't told me about it yet. I was giving you time to share it with me, but if it's a big reason that's stopping us from moving forward, from you really letting your guard down with me, then tell me about it now and maybe we can work through it together."

Melanie sighed, wondering if she should really tell Aaron about her and Andrew. She looked out the window ready to tell Aaron that she wouldn't tell him and to please take her home, but when she looked back into his warm, compassionate eyes, her mouth opened and out came the truth. "I hate having to admit this to you, but I was recently in love with my brother." She covered her eyes in shame with her hands and shivered in disgust.

Aaron sunk deeper in his seat and wiped his goatee in confusion.

Melanie peaked through her fingers trying to see how Aaron was taking what she had told him seeing as though he was eerily quiet. His hands were now laced behind his head. He stared ahead past the steering wheel, past the dashboard, out the window, at nothing at all.

"Well, say something." She kept her hands at the sides of her face as she peered at him.

"I'm not sure what to say. I mean, did you know he was your brother? Is he white, too?"

"Eww, no I didn't because if I did, I never would've dated him, and no he's not white. Why would you even think that?"

"I don't know…So help me to understand."

Melanie sighed. "Long story short, I met him through my best friend, we hit it off instantly, and were dating with talks of marriage until I found out at my best friends almost wedding that he was actually the brother my mother conceived after being raped and then eventually gave up for adoption when he was four."

"Wow."

"Yeah, wow."

"I can only imagine the emotional toil that has taken on you and not to sound insensitive, but is that the real reason, beyond race, that you don't want to be with me?"

"Yes and no."

Aaron contorted his face in confusion.

"I mean yes, because of that whole ordeal. I don't know if I can trust myself with deciding the right man for me. I mean, I thought I loved him and that we had this strong kismet connection." She looked away from him. "Ugh! I shouldn't even admit this to you now."

"What? I can handle whatever you have to say. Let's just be upfront and honest with each other. No games."

Melanie looked at him again. She was comforted by his eyes so she continued on. "What I feel for you is even stronger than the way I felt about him. How can that be when I've known you for a shorter time than I dated him? I think something is wrong with my emotional wiring."

Aaron held his side laughing at her.

"What? Don't laugh at me."

"I'm sorry. It's just the desperation in your voice and the pout on your face when you said that that made me laugh."

Melanie stuck her tongue out at Aaron.

"Okay, so if not trusting yourself to make the right decision about a man is a part of you holding back from me, is race even the issue then?"

"Yes, it's the biggest issue."

Aaron smiled, gazing at Melanie.

She could tell he was looking at her which caused her to look at him. "What?"

"Let's back track and marinate on you admitting that you like me." He smiled wide.

"Oh whatever." Melanie pressed her lips tightly together trying to hide her smile.

"And you said that what you feel for me is stronger than what you felt for a man you thought you wanted to marry." He smiled at her. "So?"

"You're white and I'm black and times like tonight remind me of why we won't work. I don't want to struggle to assert myself in this world as a woman, a black woman, and then add to that, the issue of being with you. Now will you please just take me home?" She turned her head and willed herself not to cry in front of him.

Aaron stared at her baffled before he finally put the car in drive and drove off.

***

Aaron walked into his house stumped with how Melanie admitted she was really into him, yet would continue to allow the color of their skin to dictate whether or not they could be together.

He looked down at his phone ready to call her to let her know he had made it home and try to talk some sense into her when he saw that he had missed calls and texts from Damon.

He decided to call Damon, but merely text Melanie that he had made it home.

I'm home beautiful. He pressed send.

Ok. She responded after a while.

Goodnight. Was his response back to her.

He waited for what seemed like forever when he realized that maybe she wasn't going to wish him goodnight or that she may have fallen asleep already.

He dialed Damon's number and Damon picked up on the third ring. "Yo' whaddup A?"

"Nothing man. What's up with you?"

"I'm good. But you don't sound so good. What's going on?"

"Melanie." Aaron sighed.

Damon eyebrows raised. "What's up? She still ain't feeling you?" Damon grinned.

"Man, it's crazy. She said she's into me, but we just can't be together."

"She's into you?" Damon frowned. "Whatchu doing now?"

"Sitting on my couch trying to figure out how to win her over."

Damon shook his head. "Man, she got you whipped already?" Damon chuckled.

"Yup. And I ain't afraid to admit it."

"Well, okay. How about I slide through and we come up with a plan together to get Melanie?" Damon grinned slowly, nodding his head.

"Okay. Cool man. I'm open to whatever will get me Melanie."

Damon twitched his mouth and scrunched his face. "Yeah, okay. I'm not too far away. I'll be there in like ten minutes."

"Cool."

***

"What's up, bro?" Aaron said and shook hands with Damon as he let him into his house.

"Nothing, just coming over here like I said to help come up with a plan to win Melanie over."

"Good." Aaron led Damon into the living room and they sat down on the couches across from each other. Aaron turned the sound down on the basketball game.

"Man that's messed up that Kyle Irving will probably never play basketball again. He's one of the greatest of this era of basketball." Damon shook his head.

"I know, right? But have you come up with something yet to get her to see that I really am the one for her?"

Damon smirked and slowly shook his head as he moved forward to the edge of the couch. He balanced his elbows on his knees. "How about you encourage her to go on a few dates with some other guys?"

Aaron stared at Damon.

"What?" Damon smirked at Aaron.

"I said I needed to figure out a way to get her to see that she and I are supposed to be together, but you come up with a way for me to push her into the arms of several other men? What?" Aaron fell back on the couch shaking his head in confusion as he tried to digest Damon's plan.

Damon laughed, rubbing his hands together. "Trust me, it'll work. She'll end up with the man she's supposed to be with."

14

Karen had just finished broadcasting a home game for the Bulls. She missed going to her house at night, but since Kyle had been injured she had been by his side when she didn't have to cover any games or tape her show.

She let herself into his condo with her key.

"Kyle? Kyle? Kyle?" It was pitch dark in his place and it took some time adjusting her eyesight to the inside of the condo versus the well-lit hallway she had just left, but the white tank top he had on directed her to where he was. "Get up." Karen hit him over the head with a throw pillow.

"What? Leave me alone." Kyle watched Karen as she walked over and stood at his floor to ceiling windows and opened the curtains wide. He rolled over mumbling, "Leave me alone."

"Why are you in the same spot I left you this morning?" She walked back over to where he laid and sat on the ottoman near him. "Kyle, get up."

He rolled over to face her. "No. Everything is wrong."

She moved to the edge of the couch and began to rub his back. "It's going to be okay, baby. We'll get through this. I know it hurts that the doctors said that you would never be able to play in the NBA again, but there's so much more to you than basketball."

"I wanted a ring," he mumble from under the pillow on his face.

Karen turned her head and mumbled, "I want a ring, too." She gave him a bitter smile as she turned back to face him.

"You are so charismatic and charming, you can become a broadcaster if you wanted and your IQ is so high for the game that you could be a coach at whatever level you choose. You already have so many offers." Karen tried inserting an extra dollop of joy in her voice with the last of her words.

Kyle pulled the pillow from his face.

Karen could see how vexed he was. He hadn't shaved since the news of his leg. If she wouldn't have known any better, she would have thought he was in some type of beard challenge to see which man could grow the longest and biggest beard in a matter of time. And from the looks of the locks on Kyle's face, he was in the lead.

"Kyle, you'll bounce back from this." She tried to interlace her hands with his but he pulled his hand back from her and scooted away from her on the couch.

"It's more than just never playing basketball again."

Karen grew worried. Her eyebrows furrowed and her nostrils spread.

"Mercedes called me today saying that she was ready to move back to Miami and she's taking Gabby with her."

If they were in a cartoon at that moment, one would see red smoke blaring from Kyle's nostrils and ears. He balled his fists and his shoulders tensed as he gritted his teeth.

Karen was stunned. She knew how much Kyle loved having Gabby in his life.

He grinded his teeth. "I already missed so much of her life and I finally get in it and now Mercedes wants to take my daughter away from me."

"Well, did she give you a hint that she wanted to do this before today?"

"No." Kyle's deep voice vibrated throughout the condo.

Karen didn't like the rage he was carrying.

Kyle could see the fear in Karen's eyes. "I'm not mad at you, I'm just mad with everything else. Can you give me some time alone?" He scooted back on the couch until he was able to swing his legs onto the floor. He tried to stand on both of his feet but the pain in his broken leg shot through his body and he fell back on the couch.

"Kyle, you know you can't put any weight on that leg. You have to use your crutches. And whatever you're trying to do right now, I can do it for you."

He braced his elbows on his knees and rubbed his head. "Karen, I said give me some space." He willed himself to his feet. This time he used all of his might to hop on one leg from his couch to his bedroom.

"Kyle, don't shut me out," Karen called out from the couch.

Kyle slammed the door to his bedroom behind him.

Karen tried to remain strong, but the squeak in her voice when she spoke signaled that she was holding back her tears. She grabbed her phone from her purse and pressed ten as a speed dial option.

"Hello," Mercedes said into the phone with her thick Brazilian-Portuguese accent.

"Hey. This is Karen. We need to talk."

15

"I can't believe you called Mercedes." Melanie sat at the foot of Karen's bed staring at her.

"I sure did," Karen said as she adjusted her body in the bed. "Oh, it feels so good to lay in my own bed for a change." She spread her arms out across the pillows that lined her headboard.

"Well, if you're here, who's with him?" Melanie asked.

"His mom came over to give me a break." Karen laughed. "It's not like he needs a babysitter, I mean he is a grown man, but since he's being so stubborn and prideful about doing things for himself, whenever he does get off of the couch, we've pretty much decided to be at the house 'round the clock with him."

"So why not just get a nurse for him?"

"We tried that, but he kicked her out the moment I left to go to work."

Melanie shook her head.

"Sad, I know, right? And he did the same thing with the next two nurses we hired."

"Is Mercedes a part of the rotation of care for him?"

"Nooooo ma'am. We won't be needing her services in any manner at all."

Melanie laughed. "Cut it out. You think they would ever get back together?"

Karen frowned. She paused thinking for a moment. "I know Kyle loves me. Look what he went through for us to be together, but he's so different right now. He's pushing me away more and more each day. And with Mercedes deciding that she wants to up and go back to Miami to be closer to her family, I don't know if Kyle will…" Karen's eyes watered.

"Will what?" Melanie rolled over on her stomach and propped her chin on her palms.

Karen cleared her throat before speaking, "I don't know if he will move to Miami to be with Gabby. To be with Mercedes and Gabby if he thinks that will make things better for the three of them."

"Oh, I doubt that, Karen. Kyle loves you way too much for that."

"I can't tell lately. I mean, I understand that this is major what he's going through, finding out that his basketball career is over, but—"

"Is it really over?" Melanie interrupted.

"Of course miracles can happen, but unless one does, it's over for him. I saw the x-rays. You know I know basketball and all the injuries involved with it. He can train and rehab as much as he would like, but those bones he broke and those tendons and ligaments he severed would never be truly functional again. It would hurt him so much if he tried to play even a small portion of the level he used to play."

"Wow. That's sad."

"Yeah, sad for him and for me."

Melanie furrowed her eyebrows at Karen. "This isn't about you; this is about him."

"It's about both of us." Karen pouted. "I think that Mercedes is leaving here now in hopes that since Kyle can no longer play he'll be willing to move back to Miami."

"So what, you think she wants him back?"

Karen's eyes rolled back and forth as if she were searching her thoughts for the answer to Melanie's question. "No, I wouldn't say all of that, but she may be looking at it like there's nothing to tie him down here in Chicago. But what about me?" Karen pointed at herself as tears rolled down her face.

Melanie stared at her.

"I mean, my life is here. My show, I broadcast for my favorite team in the league here. Here, here, here in Chicago."

"But you can do all of that from Miami, too."

"No, I can't, but anyway, I'm tired of being in my feelings about Kyle. I miss you. What's going on with you and Aaron? I know you still aren't letting the color of his skin get in between you two, are you? And if what you shared with Andrew is stopping you, then don't let it. You had no idea he was your brother." They both shivered in disgust and then laughed. "We have to stop that at some point."

"I try, but it just comes so natural every time I think of it." Melanie frowned.

"I know, right? But getting back to what I was saying, you can trust your heart."

"Well, ain't it the pot calling the kettle black." Melanie laughed as Karen's eyebrows lifted in confusion. "When I was trying to convince you to give Kyle a chance, you ignored your heart, followed your head, and almost ended up marrying Dennis." Melanie snarled. "By the way, have you heard from him?"

"No, not since he asked if I would cover his medical expenses after I hit him with my car the day of our wedding."

Karen and Melanie laughed.

"But seriously, Mel, from the few convos we've had a chance to squeeze into our schedules lately, I can tell in your voice and your body language that you really are into Aaron. Give it a chance. Don't let what others think affect what could really be for you."

Melanie rolled over on her back and stared at the ceiling.

"What's up? Why are you so quiet?" Karen asked as she played with one of the decorative pillows on her bed.

Melanie rolled over on her side and propped her head on her open hand.

"You're right, I do really like him, but you won't believe what he suggested I do."

"What?" Karen sat up in bed eager to hear what Melanie would say next.

"He suggested that I go on a few dates with some other guys, black and non-black, to see if I have an interest in them as strong as the one I have for him."

"Hunh?" Karen's face scrunched up.

Melanie sat up. "I know, right? How could he say he wants me, yet possibly push me into the arms of another man?"

Karen said, "Wow, this has got to be the weirdest thing I've heard in a long time. Well, other than Dennis hiring Unique and Porsha to set Kyle up."

Melanie shook her head. "Please don't rehash that memory again."

"I'm just saying, this is pretty interesting."

"Tell me about it. It has me thinking if he really likes me after all, to come up with such a dumb plan that I don't plan to follow."

Karen was silent.

"And why are you so quiet? You agree with me, right? It's a stupid plan."

"Well, the more I think about it, it's kind of genius in a crazy way."

"Really?" Melanie stared at Karen.

"Really. He knows that you two have something special. So, by helping you to see sooner than later that you two should be together, you'll finally relax and let things progress between you all." Karen smiled. "I kind of like it."

Melanie threw a pillow at her.

Karen didn't see it coming and it hit her right in the face. She took a moment to ground herself before she said, "Whatever. I'mma let that slide since you know I'm telling the truth."

"I think it's crazy. I'm not doing it." Melanie fell back on the bed and covered her face with a pillow. She pulled it tighter over her face using it to muffle her scream.

Karen laughed. "You're going to do it. You wanna prove to him that you like someone more than him, even though you know that seriously may not be the case. I can tell from the texts you send me before and after you go out with him or talk to him that you're really into him. You're gonna do it and I know just the guy to get you started."

Melanie jumped up and stared oddly at Karen.

"Yup. There's this Puerto Rican sports analyst at our Spanish sister station that I'm cool with. I know he's looking for a good woman."

Melanie bucked her eyes at Karen.

"Whatever." Karen rolled over in her bed searching for her cell phone. She found it and texted Juan.

Karen: Hola Juan. Como estas?

Juan: Hola Senorita. Soy es bueno...why are we talking in Spanish? Lol.

Karen: Because you're Hispanic! Lbs

Juan: I know that, but I speak English just as good as you...LOL. How r u?

Karen: Good. Hey, are you dating someone nowadays?

Juan: No =(

Karen: Well, I have someone you might be interested in. =)

Melanie tried to snatch the phone away from Karen, but she kept Melanie from getting it and continued texting.

Juan: Who? Is she fine?

Karen: My best friend and of course she is!

Juan: Oh. Oh yeah, I've seen her before, she is fine. ;)

Karen: Since I know you tape your show nights, are you available for a lunch date tomorrow?

Juan: Yeah, sure.

Karen: Cool. I'll text you the location and her number later. Okay.

Juan: Thanks for looking out for me Karen.

Karen: No problem. Ttyl

"I can't believe you." Melanie paced the floor.

Karen laughed. "What? Juan's a great guy, but since I already know that you're so into Aaron, you won't like Juan. I just want you to get his whole crazy idea over with so that you can move on with him."

"And why do you want that?"

"Because, you had me worried for a second after Andrew."

They both shivered and then laughed when they looked at each other.

Melanie made her way over to the wall and fell to the floor at the base of it. She pulled her knees up to her chest and wrapped her arms around her legs. She rested her chin on her knees.

Karen rolled over on her stomach with her feet kicked up in the air and rested her chin on her palms with her elbows propping her up on the bed. "I know we don't find our happiness in men or from anyone for that matter, but we're honest enough with ourselves to say that we're at the point in our lives where we want a significant other to move forward with. Build memories with, start a family with. You thought you would have that with Andrew, but when that fell apart, you kind of fell apart. Being with Aaron has seemed to put the spark back in the fiery ball that you are." Karen smiled.

"But don't you think it's too soon for me to like someone? To really get involved with a guy so soon after I was 'in love' with Andrew?" Melanie buried her face in between her knees and her chest.

"Yes and no."

Melanie looked up confused at Karen.

"Yes, we need time to completely free ourselves from the bond of one relationship before we enter another, but everyone's timeline is different. Are you still in love with Andrew?"

Melanie jumped to her feet and threw her hands on her hips. Her eyes bulged as she said, "Hellllll noooo."

Karen laughed. "Well then, if you're totally, emotionally free of Andrew then you're emotionally available to be involved with Aaron."

Melanie frowned. She slowly walked over to the bed and sat on the edge of it again.

Karen rolled over on her back to see Melanie. "So, what's still the problem?"

"Would I really be a traitor to my black brothers if I date, marry a white man? Can I handle the constant racist remarks and actions from idiots?"

Melanie fell back on the bed as she let out a loud sigh.

"Mel, the heart wants what the heart wants. You are one of the strongest women I know, so you can handle anything. And you've never let what anyone thinks dictate what you do. Well, besides your mother's feelings about men all of these years."

Melanie looked over at Karen. "Really?"

They both laughed.

"Seriously, outside of that, you've always marched to the beat of your own drum, so now that you're free from the oppression of your mother's views of men, follow your heart, and be with who truly makes you happy?"

"Ugh, I hate my life right now."

"Well, maybe your date with Juan tomorrow will change that. Let me just call him right now. He should be done at the studio by now."

Melanie tightened her stare at Karen as she held her phone up to her ear.

"You better not," she mouthed to Karen.

Karen smiled. "Hello, Juan, I figured you were done taping and decided to call you instead of texting. I have Melanie here with me now, hold on." Karen held her phone out to Melanie. "Here, Mel, someone's on the phone for you."

"I'mma get you," Melanie mouthed to Karen. She cleared her throat before she said into the phone, "Hello."

Karen fell back on her headboard laughing as Melanie made quiet threats to her.

16

Melanie sat inside a quaint Spanish restaurant on the North side of Chicago fidgeting in her chair. "Why did I agree to this blind date?" she mumbled to herself.

"Because Karen told you how great of a catch I am." Juan smiled as he came from behind her. "May I?' He pointed towards the seat across from her.

"Of course." She covered her face in embarrassment but continued speaking through her hands. "I can't believe you heard me."

"I'm glad I did. At least I know that you're as nervous as I am meeting you here like this. I've seen you a few times before with Karen at games or sports functions and I liked what I saw, but to be here with you now on a date makes me kind of nervous."

Melanie uncovered her face. She looked at him. She reconciled that his headshot on his station's website didn't serve him the justice due to him. His smooth, pecan colored, clay-like skin, dark curly hair, and bright smile could land him as the lead male character in any romance novel, but he just wasn't doing anything for her. Her breathing didn't change when she looked at him the way it did whenever she looked at Aaron.

Karen and Melanie's investigation of Juan's Facebook page didn't give them much insight into who he was personally. It was merely generic information about him as an analyst and accolades he had achieved over the years.

She would have to carefully feel him out during their date.

"So, Melanie. Tell me about yourself?"

"Well, I'm an artist. I own a gallery where I like to showcase local artists. That's pretty much me in a nutshell. Tell me something about you." She feigned a smile.

"Well, I'm a sportscaster for a Spanish broadcasting station."

"I know that. Tell me about your hobbies and whatnot."

"Well, I'm pretty much a sports head, so I enjoy doing anything sports related. How about you? You into sports?"

"No," Melanie said, hoping she didn't come off as dismissive as she felt with him at the moment. She was ready for the date to be over and it had barely started.

"Oh, I just thought you would be into sports a lot the way Karen is since she's your best friend. I mean she's really into sports and not just basketball."

"Yeah, sports is her thing, but definitely not mine. I could go without them altogether, except for running."

"Running is not a sport." Juan guffawed.

"Yeah, says someone who couldn't probably go a mile nonstop." Melanie rolled her eyes, and then stared out the window at nothing in particular.

"Okay." His eyes shifted from side to side and held his lips tight together as he watched Melanie stare out the window while she mindlessly played with the pattern on her cross-body bag. He wondered what he did wrong to cause their conversation to go sour so soon. Despite her not liking sports, which was turning out to be quite a bit of a turnoff for him, he thought she was very attractive so he was willing to make the best of the date. "So, you ready to order?"

She finally made eye contact with him again. "You know what, I'm not even hungry right now. I'll just have some water with a lemon."

Juan raised his hand to signal the waiter.

The waiter came over to the table. "Hola. Senor y Senorita, are you all ready to order?"

Juan looked at Melanie. She was looking more unhappy to him by the second. He looked back up at the waiter. "Can you give us a second?"

"Si." The waiter left the table.

"Melanie?"

She slowly looked over to him trying to hide

the annoyance she had grown for him within the short amount of time they had been in each other's presence. She raised one eyebrow as she said, "Yes?"

"Is everything okay? I feel like I'm getting a weird vibe from you right now."

Melanie looked up at him and could have sworn she saw sadness in his eyes. She bet he was confused too. "I'm sorry."

"No, it's okay. I can just order my food to go and walk you to your car."

"I'm sorry that you wasted your time coming here today."

"No." He smiled. "It wasn't a waste of my time. I got the chance to sit with a beautiful woman, even if it was brief and became awkward." They both laughed.

"You don't have to walk me to my car really. Just order your food and take care. Bye." Melanie got up from the table and walked out of the restaurant.

***

"You did what?" Karen's eyes bulged as she held the phone up to her ear using her shoulder. She struggled putting the key into the lock on the door, holding the groceries in her hand, and keeping the phone up to her ear with her shoulder.

She finally got the key to stay in the tumbler long enough to unlock the door. She managed to twist the doorknob and the door flew open from the weight of the bags in her hand. Trying not to drop the bags, her phone fell to the floor. "Melanie hold on," she screamed, hoping Melanie would hear her.

The lights were on in Kyle's condo and he sat up on the edge of the couch staring at her.

"Melanie hold on." Karen rushed to put the bags of groceries on the countertop in the kitchen and then back to the front door to get her phone off the floor and get back to talking to Melanie.

Kyle stared at her through it all. He finally spoke up by the time she made it back to the front door. "Karen, we need to talk."

She didn't hear him speak as she continued talking to Melanie. "Good, you're still there. You didn't even give him a chance. So what you're not into sports like that, I'm certain you all had other things in common."

"Karen, I said we need to talk." Kyle's voice bellowed throughout the spacious condo.

Karen snapped her neck fast to look at Kyle. The tone in his voice alarmed her and the look in his eyes let her know that he wanted to talk at and whatever the topic was wouldn't be so jovial.

She turned towards the door so that her back would face Kyle. She cupped the phone with her hand and talked low into it. "Um, I think something's wrong with Kyle. I'm gonna have to call you back later."

"What is it? Is everything okay?"

"Karen." Kyle's deep and anguished voice

sent an eerie chill up her spine.

"Mel, I gotta go." She hung up the phone while Melanie was still talking to her.

She slowly turned to face Kyle. His entire body was tense as he repeatedly balled and loosened his fists.

She eased her coat off and slowly walked over to the couch where he sat. She sat on the ottoman in front of him.

He sat quietly, but from his deep breathing, she could tell that something was off with him.

"Kyle, what's wrong? Talk to me." She reached out to grab his hand, but he pulled back from her. Unsure of what was wrong, she eased her hands into her lap.

He stared at her with anger in his eyes before he finally broke the silence in the room. "You called Mercedes?"

Obviously he knew about it, so she knew she couldn't deny it. "Well, yes, but—"

"But nothing. What, you don't think I can handle things on my own? You think I'm not man enough to carry my own weight anymore?" He stood and tried to walk off but was quickly reminded that he only had one functioning leg as he fell helplessly to the floor.

"Kyle, are you okay? Let me help you." Karen reached down to help him up but he motioned for her to stay back from him.

"I can get up on my own. I'm not helpless." He rolled over on his side and pulled himself across the floor until he was at the couch and painfully pulled himself up on it. He took a moment to catch his breath before he spoke again.

Karen stood nearby unaware of what to say or do.

"Karen, I am a man. I don't need you to handle my business for me. Just like I never asked you to be around here all the time trying to wait on me hand and foot while I deal with this injury, I certainly didn't ask you to call Mercedes and try to settle anything with her. Gabby is my daughter and I can talk for myself when it comes to discussing what's best for my child." He slammed his hand down on his good knee.

Karen was speechless. Tears welled up in her eyes as she stood wondering why Kyle was overreacting to her trying to help his situation.

"Kyle." She walked closer to him. "I know that you're a man and can handle things on your own, but I just wanted you to know that you don't have to. I got your back. Like you've had mine since day one."

Kyle slowly looked up from the ground to meet Karen's eyes. He saw sincerity in her eyes, but the pain of never playing ball again and possibly losing Gabby overcame him and blinded his compassion for Karen. "I think you should leave now. I need some time alone." He looked back down as he rubbed his head with both of his hands.

"But Kyle—"

"I said go, Karen."

Karen couldn't take the strong will in his voice anymore; his pushing her away was tearing her apart.

Tears ran down her face as she scrambled for her belongings and rushed out the door.

The doors of the elevator barely closed before she sobbed loudly.

17

Karen went home and cried herself to sleep after Kyle put her out. The pain she felt closely mirrored the gaping hole she had in her heart after she found out that her parents had died in a car crash when she was a teenager.

She was confused and hurt after he asked her to leave. She didn't understand how the same vulnerability she had to have to open up to Kyle to love him was the same vulnerability that was tearing her apart after their argument. She never meant for calling Mercedes to try and keep Gabby in Chicago to put a further divide between her and Kyle. Normally in times of trouble Melanie was the first person she ran to, but the night before, she was so numb and dazed that all she could do was pour herself into her bed and weep until sleep overtook her.

She rolled over searching for her phone to find out what time it was. She hoped Kyle putting her out the night before was all a dream and that somehow she was asleep in his bed and he on his couch like they had been sleeping since his fall on the court. But when she rolled over on her back she looked down at her clothes to see that she still had on the same outfit she had on when Kyle told her to leave his place the night before. It was her maroon comforter on her bed that was crumpled under her.

She grabbed her forehead as the excruciating pain of a headache registered with her. She moaned as she tried to sit up.

She made her way to the edge of the bed and looked down at her feet to see that she still had her boots on. She cried again knowing that she didn't fall asleep fully dressed from being exhausted but rather heartbroken when he told her to leave him alone. To her, it sounded like he really wanted her out of his life. She wasn't sure if it were for the moment or for the rest of his life. She knew she put up a lot of resistance when he first started pursuing her, but he had knocked that wall down to her heart and made it his home. The tables had turned now; she didn't want to be without him.

She made her way to the bathroom and shrieked when she looked at the wreck that was her face. Of course, her mascara from the day before streaked her face but now it had a glow to it as fresh tears streamed her face. And because she didn't tie down her short, cropped hair the night before, it was matted and wilted in ways that only her hairstylist would be able to rectify.

She wanted to mope for a while before she tried to go and salvage her relationship with Kyle before she went to tape her show. However, since she needed to add a trip to the hair salon to her schedule, she had no time to sulk at home.

She washed her face constantly pushing in the bags that had formed around her eyes from crying all night. Her nose was stuffy so she grabbed some medicine from her cabinet hoping to clear her nasal passage and voice before her show that night.

She headed to her shower and turned the water to a mild hot. She stripped down to nothing leaving her clothes in a puddle right outside the glass door of the shower.

She had thirty-two different variations to the six shower heads in her shower. She planned to use all of them hoping that with each one, it would massage away the pain her heart was experiencing.

After twenty minutes, she got out of the shower and dried off as she made her way into her walk-in closet to pick something to wear for the day.

Her face was wet, so she patted her head thinking it was water dripping from it, but when she tasted the salt water that passed her lips, she realized her tears were drowning her face.

She wanted to talk to someone to make sense of what happened the night before. She felt the only one who could do that was Kyle.

She put her lingerie on and rushed to grab her phone from off the bed. She dialed his number. No answer. She hung up again and repeated the same process and got the same results five times more.

With her sixth call, she left a voicemail. "Hi, Kyle, it's me, Karen, you know the woman you say you love." She sniffled. "Please call me back Asap. I love you…hope to hear from you soon." She ended her message and took a deep breath as more tears streamed her face.

She texted him in between texting her stylist to book an emergency appointment, but he never responded back to her.

She dialed Melanie's number and she picked up on the second ring.

"Mel," Karen sputtered into the phone.

"Karen. What's wrong?" Melanie stopped painting and stood up from her stool.

"Everything. Are you at home? I'm coming over now." Karen slipped her feet into her black Uggs near her bedroom door.

"No, I'm at my studio. I wanted to paint before I opened up the gallery. Come down here though."

"I will as soon as I come from getting my hair done."

"But you just got it done Saturday and it's only Tuesday." Melanie furrowed her eyebrows.

"Trust me, Mel, I *have* to go get it done."

"Okay. Well, come here when you can. I love you and everything will be fine." Melanie tried to sound hopeful.

"I hope so. I need it to be. I don't want to lose Kyle." Karen sniffed and wiped tears from her face as she made her way to her front door.

She put on her long down parka and grabbed her oversized shades to hide her puffy eyes before heading out the door.

***

Curiosity got the best of Karen and before she headed over to Melanie's gallery after her hair appointment, she stopped by Kyle's place.

She had called and texted him several more times since she had left home, but he never answered her calls or responded to her texts.

She soon stood at the front door to his penthouse wondering if she should ring the doorbell or use her key to let herself in. Seeing as though he hadn't responded to her yet, she thought she would have a better chance of talking to him if she should let herself in rather than wait on him to do so. She took a deep breath and put her key into the knob. It wouldn't fit. She tried inserting it every way possible, but it wouldn't fit. She squatted eye level with the tumbler to make sure she was inserting the key properly but she still had no luck with unlocking it. "I know he didn't change the locks on me that quick. And for what, because I was trying to help him?"

She fought back her tears as she rang his doorbell.

She waited for a second, but no one came to the door.

She rang it again and waited to no avail.

She was furious at this point. She didn't want to make a scene, although there was only one other penthouse on the floor and she knew the couple was away in Greece.

She banged on the door again until it slowly opened and Kyle's mother stood in the doorway.

"I'm sorry, Mrs. Irving, for making so much noise, but my key isn't working. I'm worried about Kyle. I need to talk to him." Karen stepped forward wanting to walk into the penthouse but Mrs. Irving stood in the middle of the doorway blocking access. "May I come in?" Karen's eyebrows met each other as she stared at Mrs. Irving.

Mrs. Irving eyes held so much compassion as she said to Karen, "I'm sorry, Karen, but he says he's not ready to talk to you now. He said he'll call you when he's ready."

Karen's heart sank. It was like the pit of her stomach reached up and snatched her heart from its normal spot and then they both fell to the floor. She couldn't believe he wouldn't talk to her at all. The man that made her fall in love with him. The man that took a chance interrupting her almost nuptials to a jerk just to prove how much he loved her. Now that same man wouldn't accept her calls or even let her into the penthouse they were making into a home.

She didn't want to cry in front of Mrs. Irving but her emotions were betraying her. She tried to speak again, but when she opened her mouth, no words came out. She wiped her face of tears as best as she could, put her glasses on, and headed back to the elevator.

***

"It's not funny," Melanie said as she spoke into her headset talking to Aaron.

"Yes, it is. That was one date, but how many more dates do you think you'll go on before you realize you won't feel the same way with them as you do with me?"

Melanie rolled her eyes as if Aaron could see her. "Like you said, just one date. Maybe the next one will be the one." Melanie frowned as she stood behind the counter in the gallery. A fair amount of people were now walking the floor assessing her collection.

Her assistant was running late so she had to stop painting in her studio and tend to her gallery.

"I doubt that, but of course since I challenged you to date other guys to confirm to you that I'm the one for you, then by all means, continue with your dates. I'm not worried."

"Yeah, whatever."

"Especially if they will all be like Juan."

"They better not be." Melanie laughed but her smile quickly turned into a frown when she spotted Karen walking towards the counter. Karen's oversized sunglasses were not big enough to hide the tears streaming down her friend's face. "Aaron. I gotta go. I'll talk to you later."

"What is it? Is everything alright?" Aaron stood from his desk and closed the door to his office at his store trying to understand the panic he heard in Melanie's voice.

"Yeah, I'm fine. I gotta go. Bye." She ended her call with him.

She held her arms out as Karen walked right into them. She was about a foot taller than Karen, so she looked over her head hoping that none of her patrons were staring at Karen as she was unfolding in her arms.

"Oh, honey, go to the back and grab some tissue and clean your face. I'll be back there as soon as my assistant gets here." Just as Melanie was texting her assistant, in she walked.

"Melanie, I'm so sorry." Donna took her foggy glasses from her face to clean them. "It is so cold outside and my car wouldn't start. I had to wait for someone in my apartment complex to help me jump my car."

Melanie looked at Donna with sympathy. "I've been telling you to get that car of yours fixed."

"Well, when my paintings sell like yours, then I'll be able to afford whatever car I want, but until I finish art school and sell them, me and pinto will just have to get along with each other." Donna replaced her glasses on her freckled face.

"Okay. Well, the counter is yours. Karen is in the back waiting on me. If you do need to come back there, please knock before you come in."

"Of course. Tell Karen I said hi, will ya?"

"Okay." Melanie rushed off to see about Karen.

***

"Karen? Where are you?" Melanie walked into her studio in search of Karen.

She knew exactly where Karen was when she heard the toilet flush and the creaking of the barnyard door that secured the bathroom.

"What's going on? Please come sit and talk to me." Melanie patted the empty space next to her as she sat on the loveseat against a brick wall.

Karen made her way to the couch and dropped in it allowing her head to fall into her lap.

"Tell me something. What happened? The last thing I know was that we were on the phone last night and I was telling you about my date with Juan when Kyle needed something from you. What did he want?"

"My heart." Karen took her shades off. Her eyes were bloodshot red.

"What do you mean?"

"He took my heart and crushed it last night." Karen let her head drop back in her lap as she gripped her knees and rocked herself.

Melanie rubbed Karen's back trying to comfort her. "What happened, sweetie?"

Karen talked while her head was still in her lap. "I came in ready to make him something to eat, but I didn't even get the chance to. He attacked me about going to Mercedes to see if I could convince her to stay in Chicago. He must've forgotten that he can't walk as he used to because he tried to get up from the couch to walk away from me and he fell." Karen sighed. "I tried to help him up but he demanded I get back shouting that he was a man and he could handle things on his own. He put me out. He put me out. He won't return any of my calls, respond to any of my texts, and when I stopped by to see him today, he had changed the locks."

Melanie's eyes widened at that bit of news.

"Yes, he changed the locks on me. I banged on the door until it opened."

"So he finally opened the door?" Melanie asked invested to find out what happened next.

"No. His mother did. She told me that he said he doesn't want to see me now but will contact me when he's ready. Contact me?" Karen sat up and looked into Melanie's eyes searching for understanding.

All Melanie could do was hold her arms out and hug Karen as she cried on her shoulder.

"Karen. I honestly think everything will be alright between you all. Kyle's just dealing with a lot right now."

Karen pulled back from Melanie to look at her. "But he shouldn't pull back from the one who's been supporting him day in and day out since his fall."

Melanie twisted her mouth. "Maybe that's the problem. There have been so many people around him, especially you, that he hasn't had much time to internalize this big change in his life."

"I give him space."

"No, from the way you tell it, he never really has space to himself. If you're not there, then his mother is. He probably hasn't even cried yet because he hasn't had any alone time to do so."

Karen bucked her eyes at Melanie. "Kyle? Cry? He doesn't cry. He just figures out a way to make things happen."

"Karen, be realistic. No matter how strong a person is, everyone has their breaking point. And I think the news of never being able to play b-ball was Kyle's. And then Mercedes adds the news of wanting to take Gabby back to Miami on top of that. I bet he wasn't even lashing out at you, you just so happened to be there when he was ready to release."

"But he locked me out." Karen held her hands up as if questioning Melanie.

"I know, sweetie, but that could just be his way of getting his privacy."

"But his mother was there." Karen pouted.

"And as you told me, his mother knows how to take her hands off when need be. She probably just stopped by when you did. Please don't get yourself so worked up about this. I'm certain that Kyle will reach out to you soon enough."

"And how do you know that?" Karen blew her nose.

"Because, there's no way he chased after you as hard as he did to let you go so easily. Just give him some space. I'm sure everything will work out just fine."

Karen finally smiled. "Look at us, our tables constantly turn with one another."

Melanie's eyebrows furrowed. "Mmh?"

"You had to convince me to give Kyle a chance. I'm having to convince you to give Aaron a chance and the whole dating other guys just to prove a point to Aaron thing."

Melanie shook her head. "I see your point. Do you ever think we'll get this love thing right?"

"I hope so. I only want it with Kyle though." Karen let her head drop in her lap.

There was a knock at the door. "Melanie there's a guy out here wanting to see the owner of the gallery."

"Okay. Tell him I'll be out in a minute," Melanie shouted.

"Okay." Donna walked back to the gallery floor.

Melanie turned her attention back to Karen. "How about you go and fix your face in the bathroom. Remember, you have a game to broadcast tonight and I know you don't want the zoom-ins to reflect what kind of day you've been having."

"Is it that bad?" Karen patted her face.

"It's not that bad, you've just looked waaaay better."

"Oh shut up!" Karen smiled as she headed to the bathroom.

"I'll be out on the gallery floor." Melanie called out to Karen.

***

Melanie smiled as Donna introduced her to the fine man who came in looking for her.

"Melanie, this is Damon, Damon, this is Melanie, the owner of the gallery." Donna nodded her head and walked off.

Damon smiled. "Nice to meet you, Melanie." He extended his hand to shake hers.

"And nice to meet you, too. Have we met before?" Melanie squinted, sizing him up.

"No." Damon laughed.

"So, to what do I owe the pleasure of you seeking me and my gallery out?"

"Oh, nothing. I've heard of this place before, I just never had the chance to come in here until today." He stared intently at her. "I was walking around taking in the different pieces and thought to myself that I had to meet the woman who made all of this possible." He spread his arms out wide. "Only a great mind and keen eye for good art would gather a collection like this."

Melanie squinted her eyes at him giving him her undivided attention. "So, are you an artist? Art buyer? What?"

Damon laughed. "Well, I'm a graphic design artist. I own my own design company, so I enjoy all mediums of art."

"Okay." Melanie nodded her head and smiled at him. *Not only is he fine, but he seems to appreciate art as much as I do. He's creative like me, too.* "Okay. My assistant said that you asked for me personally. How may I help you?"

"Well, word on the street is, you are the best artist in town and like I said I love art. I think it's important for us black folks, especially us entrepreneurs, to stick together and network. We never know what may come of us joining forces together."

Melanie smiled. "I agree."

"Plus, I heard that you were a cutie and I had to come see for myself." Damon winked at her.

She pursed her lips and cocked her head to the side before speaking to him. "In this day and age, if you really wanted to see how I look, you could've checked any of my social media." She folded her arms and slowly batted her eyes at him.

The dimples in his cheeks flirted with her as he smiled at her. He laughed some as he rubbed his strong jawline. "Yes, I know that's possible and I did, to be quite honest with you."

"What, so now you're stalking me? Do I need to be worried about you?" She narrowed in her stare on him.

Karen had composed herself and was now in the gallery near Melanie. She had heard all of Melanie and Damon's conversation. She thought he was cute and would be a good candidate for Melanie to go on a date with.

"I'm not stalking you, although I do admire you. After looking at your Facebook page, I decided that since I want to get to know you, I would be man enough to ask you out on a date face to face, since you made your place of employment public and invite people to visit your gallery. If that's alright with you?"

Melanie stood still. She honestly didn't know what to say; she had a gorgeous, black, educated, established man in front of her who was ready to get to know her. Although she flirted with him moments earlier, thoughts of Aaron drifted into her head.

Karen moved in closer to Melanie, but kept her back to Melanie's. She whispered as best as she could. "You heard the man. He asked you out on a date. What do ya say to that?"

Damon laughed.

Melanie tightened her lips, but then said to Damon, "Would you excuse me for a moment?" She gave him a half smile before turning to face Karen. "What are you doing? He can hear you."

"Oh." Karen held a straight face.

Melanie continued talking to Karen, "I don't know this man. He just appears out of nowhere saying he's checked out my page and wants to take me on a date and you're okay with that? He might be crazy."

"I promise you I'm not crazy and if you give me the opportunity to court you, I guarantee it'll be worth your wild." Damon smiled as Melanie's back still faced him. He stuffed his hands in his pocket as he awaited her response.

Melanie's eyes widened.

Karen laughed. "Talking about him hearing me? Apparently he can hear the both of us."

Melanie looked back at Damon again. "Excuse us for a second." She gave him a tight-lipped smile.

He nodded his head then turned to look at the piece to the right of him.

Melanie pushed Karen out of earshot of Damon.

"Why are you so tense right now? Lighten up. A fine brother practically fell in your lap and you're hesitating giving him a chance?" Karen took her shades off to make eye contact with Melanie.

"Put them back on until you get to the studio." Melanie shook her head.

"Oh whatever, but seriously, why the hesitation?"

Melanie scrunched her face in confusion.

Karen smiled. "It's Aaron, isn't it? Make up your mind. Either you're going to really give him a chance, give his plan a chance, or leave him alone all together. We've been through too much emotionally to constantly be tangled up with unnecessary emotional baggage."

"But I don't know this guy." Melanie folded her arms across her chest.

"True, but that's how you get to know him, by accepting his date. Either you're gonna find out that you like him and wanna give him a chance or that you really do like Aaron and want to start something with him."

Melanie sighed.

"One date. Give it a shot. Unless of course you already know that you want Aaron and his race doesn't matter to you after all." Karen smirked.

At the mention of Aaron's race, Melanie pivoted on her heels and headed back towards Damon.

"Damon?"

He turned towards her and smiled knowing his dimples had a hypnotizing effect on women.

She took a deep breath before speaking to him again. "Okay, I'll go on a date with you. What do you have in mind?"

18

Melanie couldn't believe where she was as Damon held the door open to the paint and sip shop she had been to weeks before with Aaron.

Tonya smiled as Melanie walked through the door. "Melanie, you're back!" She reached out to hug and air kiss Melanie hoping the two of them had become that familiar with one another.

Melanie half smiled at Tonya as she accepted her embrace. "Nice to see you again too, Tonya."

Tonya looked past Melanie to see Damon smiling and standing close to Melanie as if they were indeed on a date. She leaned in close to whisper to Melanie. "And I see you're here with a different guy this time, so hopefully you won't have the same problem you had last time and I can actually get a painting from you." Tonya smiled and hugged Melanie again.

"Tonya, the hugging." Melanie tried to keep an air of joviality in her voice.

"Oh, I'm so sorry, Melanie. It's just that I'm such a huge fan of yours. I feel like I know you through your art work. I just love you. I'm sorry, but let me get you checked in and escorted to your easels."

"Thanks." Melanie smiled.

Melanie and Damon followed an employee to their painting space.

Damon helped Melanie take her coat off. "What was that all about?" He laughed.

"Oh, I was here recently and there was a problem with some other patrons, but the owner, Tonya, handled it well for me."

"I'm sorry, I didn't know that you had been here before. Although I know you're an artist, I thought I was surprising you bringing you here. If you like we can go somewhere else."

"No, that's fine."

"Well, I hope I can make your experience here tonight better than the last one." Damon smiled, knowing exactly what happened with her and Aaron since Aaron had told him about it. He planned to take her everywhere Aaron had taken her and create happy and memorable experiences with him there. He wanted to show her that she belonged with a black man, him, and not Aaron.

"I hope so, too."

Tonya came over and offered Melanie and Damon some of her premium wine. They accepted it and continued to chat while waiting for the class to begin.

"So Damon, tell me more about you."

"What, the stuff that you didn't find out from my Facebook page?" Damon laughed.

Melanie's eyebrows furrowed as if she were offended at what he said. "What? I haven't checked your Facebook page."

"You do know they have that app to tell who's looking at whose page, right?"

"Oh, that thing actually works?" Melanie bit her lip nervously.

"Yes, it does." Damon smiled.

Melanie stared at him for a second before they both exploded in laughter. Her stint of laughter ended in holding his arm to help her regain her balance on her stool. *My gawd! His muscles are really firm.* She wanted to hold his arm longer, but opted against it and rejoined their conversation. "Okay, I admit, I checked your social media, but I had to find out who I was going on a date with tonight. We just met yesterday, so it's not like we've had lots of phone convos for me to get a better feel of you." She stared at him as if he better had accepted her explanation. "And besides, you did the same thing to me." She laughed.

"True."

Tonya stood on a platform showing the piece that everyone would emulate. She also took her time up there to give tips on how to achieve the finished look.

Smooth music filled the room and everyone began painting while sipping on wine and conversing with those they came with.

"Wow, she really is wired, isn't she?"

Melanie laughed. "Yeah, she is, but she's nice. At least that's what I gather from her seeing this is only the second time I've met her."

"Okay, so do you get mauled by fans like that on the regular?" Damon stared at Melanie.

"No." She giggled. "And would you stop staring at me like that."

"Like what?"

"I don't know, like the way you are."

"What, with pure interest in you? I wanna know everything about you. You can tell me some things, but some things I just have to observe." His stare continued to penetrate her being.

She turned her attention back to her canvas trying to redirect her thoughts. His stare was nerve wrecking, but his dimples comforted her all at the same time. "So, tell me some more about you, and here, if you want to achieve the same look as the model painting, for the waves in the water, you have to stroke the canvas like this." She grabbed his hand and guided his strokes.

He stared at her instead of the canvas as she gripped his hand.

She took a deep breath blushing. "Damon, would you focus already?"

"I am focusing, on you that is."

"I'm not the subject of interest right now. Your painting should be."

He grabbed the brush from her hand and gently caressed her hand as he said to her, "Anytime we're together, you'll always be the subject of interest for me." He lifted her hand to his lips and placed a gentle kiss on the back of her hand.

She smiled, slowly pulling her hand from his grasp.

He smirked remembering how Aaron had told him that kisses on the back of her hand seemed to captivate her. His plan was to do what she liked, but better than Aaron, make her forget that Aaron ever existed.

Melanie pulled her eyes from Damon's and tried to lock them on her painting. She hated to admit it, she really was fond of Aaron and loved the way he made her feel when they were alone and on the phone, and even when they ran into racist people in public. Aaron's presence comforted her no matter what, but now she sat there becoming more comfortable with Damon and enjoying the subtle and overt things he did to let her know he liked her. She needed a sign and soon as to what guy, if any, she would end up with.

"So tell me more about you, Damon." She looked in his direction but quickly looked back to her painting.

He looked at her and smiled seeing how hard she was working to keep her eyes off him. They shifted in his direction so many times, but when she realized he was looking at her she quickly looked back at her painting.

"Well, you already know what I do for a living. I was born and raised in Chicago. A two-parent home. The only child."

"Oh, just like me." Melanie's eyebrows furrowed. "Well, not anymore."

"Hunh? Did your parents just have a child or something?"

"No."

"So how is it not anymore?"

She looked at him. "It's a long story, and not one I care to share."

"Well, hopefully you'll open up to me about it one day."

With a pensive expression on her face, she looked at him. "Or maybe not."

"Yeah, we'll see."

She stared at him longer looking to see if his eyelashes danced with his eyelids as Aarons did, a sight that always intrigued her, but when she saw they didn't, she looked away from him.

"So, tell me more. How was it growing up for you? Ever been married before? Kids?"

He laughed at her barrage of questions. "Growing up for me was great. I have a close-knit family with strong values and morals. I loved watching my mother and father's relationship as I was growing up. Black love at its best." He stopped painting and looked at her again. "I want the kind of love they had, still have. Black love."

Melanie shook her head at herself. So far, Damon was everything that she could want in a man and yet her mind continued to drift to Aaron. *Maybe the more time I spend getting to know Damon, the less I will think about and like Aaron. I mean Damon is*

fine, his own boss, educated, aware of black love.
She laughed out loud at her last thought.

"What's funny?"

"Oh, nothing."

"So, tell me about you?"

"Well, as I told you, I'm an, well was, only child. Both of my parents have always been around, no matter how strange that relationship was."

"Hunh?"

"Oh nothing."

"That's the second thing you've dismissed when talking to me. Clearly, I have some work to put in to get you to see you can trust me, and I'm willing, Melanie. I really like you."

Melanie grimaced and scrunched her face. "How can you say you really like me and we just met yesterday?" Melanie turned to face him on her stool.

He turned to her giving her his undivided attention. "Because I do." He smiled.

"How so?"

"It doesn't take a man long to know if he wants no term, short term, or long term with a woman." He could tell he had intrigued her. "See, when a man is mature and honest with himself, he's already figured out what type of woman he wants long term in his life, in my case, a wife. So when I read your profiles, talked with you yesterday, on the phone last night, and being here with you now, I'm convinced I want you." Damon stared directly at Melanie.

She turned her attention back to her painting.

"Why do you keep doing that?"

"Doing what?" Melanie blended the water more thoroughly on her painting.

"Not look me in my eyes? Afraid you might see something you don't want to see?"

"Hunh?"

"Afraid you might see that we really do have a connection?"

"And why would I be afraid of that, if that is the case?"

"Because I can tell that you're the guarded type. Granted you should be in the beginning until you really feel comfortable to let your guard down with a person, but I sense you're being extremely guarded. If you never really give me a chance, you'll never see that I'm just right for you."

Melanie laughed. "Full of ourselves, aren't we?"

"No, just confident and sure of what I want."

The hairs on the back of Melanie's neck stood up. She had heard that exact phrasing from somewhere else, she couldn't remember from where though.

"Look, Damon, you are a great guy from what I've seen of you thus far. I'd rather be safe than sorry and take things slow. I don't want to rush something between us and it not get either of us the end results we want."

"Which is what?" Damon asked.

"Hunh?"

"What's your end result for a relationship?"

"To get married, have kids, love each other unconditionally, grow old together."

He smiled. "Well, I want those things too, and from what my eyes see and what I'm sensing, I want all of that with you."

She gave him the side-eye. "But it's only been one day."

"One day to you, but a lifetime for me. I've been wanting you for a long time."

"But we just met." Melanie shook her head amazed.

"Sometimes we meet people before we ever meet them face to face," Damon mumbled as he focused on his painting.

19

Marie rolled over onto her back. She took deep breaths trying to slow her heart beat. She looked over and smiled at Howard who was smiling at her.

"You haven't stopped since we started that day I first saw you again." He laughed.

Marie rolled over on her side and propped her head on her hand as she talked to him. "I know. I mean, I didn't get the chance to really enjoy you as my husband when we were married, but now," she leaned forward and pecked him on his lips, "now I can." She kissed him deeper.

"But we're not married now."

"I know." She rolled on her back again. "Why'd you have to mention that?" She pouted.

"Because I know you honor marriage and you know I do. You know I never stopped loving you over the years. I won't say I married my wife because I was settling, because we were good for each other. But now that I have you back in my life, I want you back in it as my wife." He saw her body tense up. He pulled her into his arms. "No need to tense up. You're different now. And now that I know what it was that kept us from being as close as we could've, I know how to love you better."

"It wasn't you, Howard, it was me." Tears warmed her face. Her dark almond skin glowed despite her mood. "And I'm sorry for being that way with you."

"It's okay. That's the past. Let's just move forward, together."

"But what about Melanie? What do you think she will say?"

Howard laughed. "What about Melanie? I think she'll love the idea of us being married again."

"I hope so. She better, because it's going to happen." Marie cooed and winked as she mounted Howard.

"Well, I'm glad we took a break to talk so I could recharge my battery."

"Me, too."

Howard kissed her passionately as he gripped her gyrating butt.

The doorbell rang.

They stopped moving.

"Are you expecting company?" Howard asked.

"No. Maybe it's the mailman or something. They'll get the hint when I don't open the door." Marie leaned down and allowed her mouth to cover Howard's as his hands roamed her slightly plump body.

The doorbell rang again and this time the person at the door seemed to have their finger glued to it. The person didn't let up off it.

Marie rolled her eyes and took a deep breath. "Let me go and get rid of whoever is at the door. I'll be right back to you, superman." She winked.

"I like it when you call me that."

Marie pried herself away from him and jumped out of bed. She grabbed her robe and closed the door behind her.

She descended the stairs and looked through the peephole. She quickly stepped away from the door to look at the mirror on the wall. She smoothed her hair out as best as she could and tightened the belt on her robe. She cleared her throat and opened the door. "Andrew, it's so good to see you. What are you doing here?" Her voice shook in nervousness.

Andrew paused searching for a reasonable explanation for showing up at her house. "Nothing much, I was just in the neighborhood and I wanted to see you."

Marie smiled. "Drew, in the neighborhood? You live downtown, this is Westchester. There's not much around here to get in to. What do you really want?" She kept her warm smile on her face. The frigidness that was still in the air ripped through the house. "Come in, it's cold out there." She looked towards the stairs hoping Howard wouldn't come down with her having been gone away from him for so long. No one knew they were back together yet.

Andrew stepped in the house and wiped his boots on the mat at the door. "I like when you call me Drew."

Marie opened her arms and pulled him into her embrace. She kissed his cheek, but the coldness of his coat made her shiver.

"Sorry."

"It's okay. Now what really brings you by here?" Marie hesitantly escorted him to the couch. Although she really did want to get back to Howard as soon as possible, she vowed to herself a while back that she would always make time for Andrew whenever he came by or called her. She owed him that much, and she enjoyed being around him, too. She missed much of his life up to that point, but wouldn't miss a second more. "Is everything okay?" She looked into his eyes as she gripped his hand.

He smiled as he saw how much concern she had for him, something he always wanted from his birth mother. "Yes, everything is fine. I really was passing through here on my way to Oakbrook and I wanted to see you. I know I showed up unannounced, and I'm sorry for that, but I really did wanna see you."

"Oh." She pulled him into a hug. She kissed his cheeks and then pinched them.

Andrew blushed, laughing.

"So what's new with you?" *Please let Howard stay upstairs until Drew leaves.*

"Nothing much. My dad will be retiring this year, and I'm busy planning a surprise retirement party for him. My siblings pitch in sometimes with it, but with them having families and careers of their own, they figured the single child, me, could handle it all on my own. My mom tried to help but she's never been the party planning type, even for our birthdays growing up, my dad planned our parties. That's the reason why I haven't hired a party planner, if he made time in his busy schedule to make our days special, then the least I could do is to put in the leg work to make his day special and specific for him. So it's all on me."

Marie's shoulders slumped some.

Andrew noticed the shift in her mood. "Oh, I'm sorry, Ma. I mean you're my mother, but she is, too."

Marie wiped a tear from her eye. "It's okay, Drew. It really is." She patted his hand. "I gave you up, so it's only fair that you respect the people that raised you, your real mother and father."

"Yes, they were great to me, still are, and I will always love them for that, but you're my real mother."

Andrew hugged Marie. He held on to her before she finally pulled away from him. "Sorry for getting emotional on you. I think it's great that you all are planning the party to celebrate your father's career."

"Yeah, I would love for you and Melanie to come to it. You know, finally meet them. You can always meet them sooner if you'd like, but I figure the party would be a light-hearted occasion to do so."

"Sure. I'd love to meet them, but I think we still have some more work to do on Melanie."

"Melanie's a great and kind woman. She'll come around soon enough." Andrew was hopeful.

"I hope so. Anything else going on in your life? Gonna give me some grandbabies anytime soon?" Marie raised her eyebrows in hope.

"I wish, but not yet. But my other sister did just have her baby. Wanna see the pics?"

"Sure."

Andrew pulled his phone out and went to his media gallery. The first pic of the baby was of his father holding her.

Marie glimpsed at the screen as Andrew zoomed in on the baby. She covered her gaping mouth in sheer horror.

"See, isn't she beautiful. Her name is—"

"Drew, can you shrink the picture again?" Marie gripped the edge of the base pillow on the couch.

"Sure, you can't see the baby as good on it when I do, but okay."

Andrew shrunk the picture down to its original size.

Marie's fingernails pierced Andrew's skin as she gripped his hand.

"Ma, what's wrong?" Andrew looked up at Marie noting the ghastly look on her face. Her eyes were wide, tears pooled them, and her chest heaved up and down from her sporadic breathing.

"No! No! No!" Marie retreated to the corner of the couch gripping a throw pillow closely to her.

"Ma, what's wrong?" Andrew reached out to calm her but her hands turned into human pinwheels flailing at him. She screamed.

"Ma."

Howard raced down the stairs with nothing but his boxers on. He rushed to Marie's side.

Andrew's face contorted into even more confusion.

Marie was still screaming until she felt Howard's hands around her. He pulled her into him. "Shhh. Shhh. It's okay. Whatever it is, we'll get through it together. I'm not going anywhere."

Although Andrew had never met the man consoling Marie before, judging from his facial features, he gathered the man must be Melanie's father. He cleared his throat to speak. "I don't know what happened, sir, but one minute we were looking at a picture and the next minute she was screaming no."

Marie continued to whimper in Howard's arms.

Howard said, "It's okay, son. I think it's best you leave now."

"But—"

"It's okay. I know who you are. Once I get her calmed down, either I'll call you and update you on her or if she's ready to talk to you, she'll call you." Howard kissed the top of Marie's head.

Andrew stood still. He wasn't ready to be pushed out of Marie's life again.

Howard saw the sincere concern for Marie in Andrew's eyes. Howard smiled as best as he could, given the circumstances. "It's okay, son. I promise I'll call you before the day is over."

Andrew turned to walk towards the door, but then turned around again to face Howard. "But you don't have my number."

"I'll either get it from Marie or from my daughter. I'll call you."

Andrew slowly walked towards the door. He opened it then looked back at the whimpering Marie.

Howard looked over to Andrew when he didn't hear the door close. "Son, everything's gonna be alright. I'll call you."

***

Melanie stared at her phone as she laid on her couch watching Netflix movies. It was her lazy day. She didn't feel like going down to the gallery and she was glad that she had an assistant that could be trusted to run it the way she liked in her absence.

She put the phone down face flat on her stomach, that way it would stop ringing, but Andrew wouldn't be wise to the fact that she wasn't answering her phone.

She smiled getting back into the plot of the movie she was watching when a flood of texts came through.

She paused *Mr. Wright* starring Queen Latifah and Common to check her messages. She jumped up barely reading them. All she saw was Andrew saying their mother was freaking out and she needed to answer her phone. Although she had barely spoken with her mother lately while her mother was trying to build a bond with Andrew, she still loved her mother with all that was in her. She knew, or at least thought she knew, that her mother hadn't had any more episodes since Andrew had been around. She'd learned from a phone conversation with her mother recently that she'd started back seeing her sisters and brothers again. She even recalled her mom telling her that she was back on speaking terms with her dad. *What does Andrew know about my mother that I don't?* She rushed into her room looking for clothes to put on as she dialed Andrew's number. She still knew it by heart. She shuddered.

He picked up on the first ring.

"Drew?"

"You both call me that." He smiled. His adoptive family called him Andrew or oddly Andy when they were joking with him.

"What?" Melanie put her socks on her feet.

"Nothing."

"Boy, what is wrong with my mother?" She jumped as she pulled her jeans up over her hips.

"Our mother."

"Whatever." Melanie rolled her eyes wishing Andrew could see her facial expression.

"I just pulled up in front of your building. Will you let me in when I buzz?"

"No, I need to go see my mother. I don't have time for you right now."

"Mel, let me up and let's talk before we go back over there together."

"We? Back over there? Drew, tell me what's going on." Melanie stood still in her room.

"Your father is there with her so she was calming down when I left. If you'll let me up, I can tell you what happened."

"My father's there with her? What, did he come while you were there?"

Andrew laughed. "Um—"

Melanie cut him off before he could speak. "What's funny, Drew?" She was growing more and more irritated with him by the minute.

Andrew stifled his laughter to speak. "Actually, he came running from upstairs with nothing but boxers on when she started screaming."

"Boxers? Screaming? I'm on my way over there."

Her doorbell rang.

"I'm in the lobby, just let me up. I'll tell you what I know and then you can decide if we should still go back."

Melanie rushed to her front door to unlock it. "My code for the elevator is still the same. Use it and come on up. The door will be unlocked."

She rushed back into her room to grab a sweater and her boots.

She heard her door open and close. She walked into her living room anxious to hear what Andrew had to say about her mother, but still not ready to interact with him. The distance she had been keeping between the two of them was perfectly fine with her.

"Hey." He waved at her and gave her a half grin. He really wished that she could just get past what they once were, and move on to who they were at that point—sister and brother.

"Yeah, hey." She faked a smile. "So what's going on with my mother? Why were you there?" She slipped the sweater over her head.

"Again, she's my mother, too and she told me I could stop by and see her anytime I wanted, so I did."

"So just you stopping by, made her scream and have an episode? Was she scratching herself?" Melanie sat down to put her boots on.

"No, but she got me pretty good." Andrew looked down at the cuts on his hand and then held it out to show Melanie.

She looked for a moment. "You'll live." She walked past him to grab her scarf.

"Melanie, would you slow down for a second and hear me out?" He tightened his jawline and talked through clenched teeth.

Melanie heard the distress and determination in his voice. With a raised eyebrow, slowly she turned from her coat rack and looked at him. "Okay."

"As you asked earlier, but wouldn't let me finish telling you…"

Melanie threw up her hands as if she were surrendering to letting him have his moment. Her oversized sweater finally fell in place on her body.

"She looked kind of disheveled when she opened the door, but I didn't say anything about it to her." Andrew smirked.

"What do you mean disheveled? Is there something you're not telling me?"

Andrew laughed. "Calm down, I'm just trying to tell you how I saw it." He muffled his laughter. "Disheveled like she'd just gotten out of bed."

Melanie's eyebrows furrowed.

"Anyway, she let me in and we were sitting on the couch talking. She asked me what was new with me, so I started sharing with her how my other family and I was planning my dad's retirement party."

Melanie smiled. "Oh, how is he? The rest of your family?"

"They're good. They miss you."

Melanie frowned. "Will you continue about my mother?"

Andrew gave Melanie a stern side eye.

"Okay, *our* mother…"

Melanie slowly rolled her eyes at him still wishing she didn't have to acknowledge the fact that he was her brother.

"You know, you never used to roll your eyes or have such a sassy and nasty attitude before."

"Well, sometimes the things we go through in life changes us."

"Yeah, but it should be for the better, not let them make you bitter."

"Whatever. This isn't about me. What about my… our mother?"

"I told her that my oldest sister just had her baby."

"Aww, I'm so happy for her and her husband."

Andrew smiled before continuing to speak. He was happy to see the nice side of Melanie amidst her rage for him at times. "The first pic in my gallery was of my dad and the baby. I zoomed in trying to let her get a closer look of the baby, but she demanded that I return the pic to its regular size. When I did, she looked at it for a second and then went into one of her 'episodes' as you say."

Melanie's eyebrows furrowed. "So who was on the pic again?"

"Just my niece and my dad. I know my niece is not ugly and she's never met my dad before."

Melanie shook her head at Andrew.

"What?"

"I see you haven't lost your sense of humor saying you know the baby didn't scare her."

"I wasn't trying to be funny though." He smiled, realizing that Melanie was relaxed with him for the moment.

"Anyway, since it wasn't the baby, and we know she's never met your dad, I wonder if it were something in the background to freak her out?"

"Let's see." Andrew pulled his phone out.

Melanie went closer to him and they studied the picture together.

Melanie stood with her hands on hips. "I mean, there really is nothing in the background but a chair. That wouldn't have made her freak out the way she did."

Melanie went over to her couch and fell back on it allowing her hands to cover her face.

Andrew sat on the arm of the loveseat across from her. "What's wrong?"

Keeping her face covered, she said to Andrew, "Nothing's wrong. I just know that I've spent much of my life running to her rescue whenever she had an episode." She sat up to look at Andrew. "How was she again when you left?"

"She wasn't screaming, just crying in your dad's arms."

"Good then. I won't rush over there yet. I'll find out later why she looked disheveled as you say she did and why my dad was coming from upstairs with nothing but his boxers on. He being there with her should be good enough, I mean she hasn't called me." Melanie reached for her phone from the ottoman in front of her. "See, no calls from her. I'm normally the one she calls in distress, but I guess whatever it was is not so bad at all."

"I guess."

"Well, thanks for informing me about *our* mother, but if you don't mind, I'd like to get back in my pj's and get back to *Mr. Wright*," Melanie said.

"Hunh? Is that what you're calling ole boy you told us about at dinner that night?"

Melanie laughed. "No, the movie *Mr. Wright* starring Queen Latifah and Common."

"Oh." Andre laughed. "But what about that guy?"

Melanie smiled.

"Looks like you really like him."

"Yeah, but I have a problem. Well, more than one now."

"I'm all ears." Andrew fell back onto the couch.

Melanie rolled her eyes contemplating if she really should let Andrew into her personal life. She remembered how good of a listener he was so she decided to open up some to her brother. She shuddered.

He shook his head. "You still do that when it comes to me."

"Some habits die hard."

"I see." Andrew laughed.

"Well, I really do like Aaron, that's the white guy, but that's the problem, he's white."

"Mel, you're better than that. Don't let the color of a person's skin determine how you interact with them."

"Trust me, I try not to, but with the constant racist encounters we've had when we're together, him being white really is a problem with me."

"But do you like him?"

Melanie twirled strands of her hair. She paused searching her heart. "I really do."

"So let love win."

"I didn't say I loved him, I said I liked him."

"Mel, although you don't admit it, you don't just like people. To talk about him as you have, smile the way you do, you more than like him."

"Yeah, that may be true, but I'm really starting to like this other guy, too."

Andrew sat up. "Other guy? No sister of mine will be a hussie." Andre laughed.

Melanie threw a throw pillow at him.

"Seriously, Mel, one guy at a time. Women aren't like dudes. Sad to say, but we can date multiple women at one time and not be attached to any of them. Y'all aren't like that."

"Oh whatever. I don't want to date two guys at once, but it was Aaron's idea. I went along with it to prove a point to him."

"What idea?" Andrew's eyebrows raised.

Melanie sat up. "Well, as I said I really do like, care for Aaron, but after so many dates with him where it was clear interracial dating wasn't accepted at the locations we went to and by the patrons there, I had to tell him that we couldn't move forward because of our races. But because he's certain we're right for each other, he dared me to go on dates with some other guys to see if I will connect with any of them the way I do with him."

"And you agreed to that?" Andrew shook his head astonished.

"I didn't want to, but I did. So what?"

"Doesn't seem like something you would do. Dumb move on his part, but I guess in an odd way I can see why he wanted you to do it. If you alls connection is real and strong, then no one could sever it."

"Yeah, but someone may have." Melanie covered her face with a pillow.

"What do you mean?"

"Well, the first guy I went out with was totally not my type, but then this guy, Damon, came along recently. He's black, a plus, and he just seems to know exactly what I like." Her lips slowly curved into a smile.

"Okay, so what will you do?"

"I don't know. That's my problem."

"Just trust your heart."

"I don't think I can." Melanie sighed. "It had me thinking you and I would get married one day." She shuddered.

"Whatever. Let's just let the past be the past. Trust your heart."

"I hope I can in time."

Silence blanketed the room for a minute, before Melanie decided to speak up.

"What's wrong with you? Still thinking about *our* mother?"

"Yeah, but not about today. I just really wish she would tell me who my father is."

Melanie looked at him. "Drew, I know how much and for how long you've wanted to know your birth parents, but you have your birth mother in your life now. Enjoy her and when and if she's ready to tell you who the lowdown dirty dog is, then she will." Melanie's eyebrows drew closer together as a sign of her confusion. "And why do you wanna know who he is anyway given what he did to her?"

"I know this may sound weird to you, but despite how they conceived me, he's still my father. He may have other kids. I wanna know his mom, my grandma. If I have any more brothers and sisters. Just like I know you, I wanna know them. That's why I'm glad you let me in tonight. I'm glad we've had the chance to talk. It's good to see you warming up to me as your brother, but I need a favor from you."

"What now?" Melanie sighed.

"Help me convince our mother to tell me who my biological father is."

20

Melanie had been seeing both Aaron and Damon equally over the past couple of weeks which was making her more confused about which one she would go further with.

That night she was going on a date with Damon. She stood in front of the mirror in her bathroom readying herself. She twisted the strands of her hair trying to make each coil perfect. She smiled thinking on how both Aaron and Damon seemed to love her natural hair.

She pouted thinking about how she really hadn't been spending as much time with Karen as they used to. They texted often, but not much face to face contact. Melanie knew that since Karen was still in what seemed like limbo with Kyle, she had buried herself in her work. She not only traveled with the Bulls to broadcast their games, she also taped her weekly show, as well as agreed to make guest appearances on a lot of sports shows. She was glad that Karen kept busy to keep from being so down about Kyle's withdrawal from her, but she missed her friend.

She turned the volume up on the radio in her bathroom and danced as Corrine Bailey Rae's "Girl Put Your Records On" filled the room with a sultry yet mid-tempo beat. She grabbed her hairbrush to use as a microphone and began to dance as if she were putting on a concert for her fans. She danced and smiled without caution.

"You never really did have rhythm," Karen said loudly over the music.

Melanie jumped, clutching her chest. She turned her nose up to face Karen. "Oh whatever! You just wish you had my moves."

"Then I'd be rhythm-less like you." Karen stuck her tongue out.

"Don't sneak up on me like that again." Melanie wagged her finger at Karen. "But I'm glad you did. I miss you." Melanie ran to Karen and threw herself at her.

Although Karen was leaning against the wall with her arms folded at her chest, the weight of Melanie's movement was too much for her to bear. She lost her balance causing both of them to fall to the floor.

They laughed.

"Why'd you do that?" Karen snarled playfully. "You could've really hurt me, yourself too."

"I knew you'd break my fall." Melanie laughed.

Karen pushed Melanie off her, but Melanie held on tight.

"Get off me," Karen mumbled as Melanie squished her face with hers, hugging her.

"No, I've missed you so much." She kissed Karen's cheek one last time before finally getting off her.

Smiling, Melanie jumped up and onto her feet.

Karen sat up straight and wiped at her face pretending to wipe Melanie's kisses from it. "Ewww, with you dating two men at the same time, I don't know where your lips have been." Karen laughed.

Melanie cocked her head and smacked her lips at Karen. "Really? You know me better than that."

"Yeah, I know you, but I know under certain conditions, we do things we normally wouldn't do."

"Like what?" Melanie stared incredulously at Karen.

"I don't know. Maybe in your quest to see which guy you like better, you may have kissed them both already."

"Nope. Not me. Although I have thought about doing that to be the determining factor, but I don't wanna kiss two different guys back to back. Enough about me. How are you? What's up with you and Kyle?"

Karen frowned.

Melanie could see water puddling in Karen's eyelids at the mention of Kyle.

"He still won't see me, but he does text me good morning or good night every now and then."

Melanie furrowed her eyebrows. "Really? That's all?"

"Yup." Karen wiped the tears from her face. "But I don't wanna be sad now, so let's change the subject. What are you getting ready to do?"

"Go out with Damon." Melanie winked.

***

"You look amazing," Damon whispered to Melanie as he helped her take her coat off.

It was the end of black history month and he had taken her to yet another black pride event. The night would be filled with poetry, comedy, and singing.

"Thanks." Melanie smiled at him as they took their seats in the middle of the auditorium.

"We sure have gone to a lot of black history events this month, not that I have a problem with it though."

"Yeah, I think it's important for us to understand where we came from in order to better prepare for where we need to go as a people. But I'm certain you already know that since you did minor in African American studies."

Melanie smiled. "Yeah. I just wish more of our people would embrace our history three hundred and sixty-five days of the year, rather than the twenty-eight the government allots for us annually."

"Yeah, well, that's up to people like us, strong couples like us, to continue to push that agenda."

"Couples like us?" Melanie raised one eyebrow, staring at Damon.

He grinned. "Yeah, couples like us. I know we haven't had the official talk yet, but we talk daily, see each other at least three times out of the week, and you know how I feel about you. I thought it was understood we're exclusive."

Uh, nah bruh, not exclusive since I see and talk to Aaron as often as I do you. She conjured up a smile before speaking. "No, I don't assume anything when it comes to men. You would literally have to ask me to be your woman and I consent before I acknowledge us as a couple."

"Well, excuse me." Damon feigned being offended.

"Oh whatever. I wasn't trying to offend you or anything." Melanie patted his hand and laughed.

He grabbed hers and gently kissed the back of it.

"I know you weren't." He stared into her eyes as he planted more kisses on the back of her hand.

Melanie was stumped. She hadn't made up in her mind if she liked it better when Aaron kissed her hand like that or when Damon did. She looked around the room to see that everyone was chatting and smiling with the people they came with waiting for the show to begin. She was saddened thinking of all the negative comments she would have heard or the downright disrespectful looks she would have gotten had she been there with Aaron. *I miss him.*

Things with Damon when they were out together flowed smoothly, no issues with her being with him as a black man. She enjoyed that.

Damon was fine and had all of the qualities she wanted in a man, but her heart literally skipped a beat when her thoughts migrated back to Aaron. The way he smelled, the way he said her name, the way he played in her hair, the way he kissed her hand. *Yeah, I definitely like his kisses better.* Everything about him was so genuine to her.

She looked over at Damon surfing Facebook on his phone. *Aaron always gives me his undivided attention whenever we're together. We never even touch our phones. The conversation is nonstop, unless we're at something we have to be quiet at, and even then, we whisper to each other often. But Damon and I do have a lot of things in common. I mean oddly, a lot of things in common. It's like we grew up together. I'm not even sure I've told him about some of the stuff he seems to guess and know about me. Is he really that into me that he just gets me without fail?* She looked at him again still on his phone. She frowned. *His eyelashes don't tickle his eyelids in the quirky way Aaron's does.*

She giggled at herself.

Damon looked up from his phone. "What's funny?" He smiled at her.

"Nothing."

He smiled at her then kissed the back of her hand he was still holding onto. She scrunched her nose in annoyance at the gesture.

The lights dimmed in the auditorium and the host took the stage.

Damon put his phone away. He leaned over and kissed her cheek.

Melanie was stunned but didn't say anything to him. *His lips are fairly soft. I guess I could get used to them.*

***

Melanie walked through her front door smiling. She ended up enjoying her date with Damon, except for something he said to her on the way home. She had never told him about it. In fact, Karen and Aaron were the only ones she had shared that thought with.

She frowned. *So how did he know?* She shrugged her shoulders. *Maybe it's just one of those things that he just gets about me.* She abandoned her thoughts and went into her bathroom to shower.

She was putting on her pajamas when she heard alerts on her phone. She rushed to get it and saw that Aaron had called her. She smiled reading his texts asking if she were okay. She felt kind of bad that she was about to call Aaron back even though she had just went on a date with Damon. *But so what! Dating other guys was Aaron's braniac idea anyway.* She did kind of feel bad for Damon though. He didn't know she was seeing Aaron; he thought the two of them were exclusive.

She knew she needed to make a decision soon. She didn't want to hurt either of them. *Shoot, I don't wanna hurt myself. I'm starting to feel like LeToya Luckett when she wrote that song "Torn".*

Melanie looked back at the picture of her and Aaron in her phone for his contact info. It was a really cute picture of them. She felt butterflies in her stomach knowing she was about to talk to him and she was glad that she hadn't kissed Damon on the lips as he had tried when he dropped her off. She wasn't ready to kiss either of them. *Although I am looking forward to kissing Aaron if we end up together. I can imagine him rubbing my head as he kisses me. Feeling his eyelashes flutter against my face as we share a passionate kiss.* She laughed at her inner thoughts as she plopped down on her bed and pressed call for Aaron.

"Aaron?"

"Hey, beautiful. How are you?"

"I'm good."

"I miss you. I called you back to back tonight hoping to hear your voice."

Melanie smiled. His voice was so smooth yet rugged to her. Its deep timbre had the perfect blend of pure sensuality and manliness.

She hesitated telling him where she was, but since it was his plan, she figured it wouldn't bother him. "Um, Aaron, I went out with that guy again tonight."

Aaron frowned. "The same one for about a month now?"

He sounded dejected to her.

"Yeah." She held her breath waiting to hear what he would say next.

"So, do you know how you feel about him versus me now?"

"It's only been a month with him. I can't know that by now."

"Yeah, but it's been like three with me. And I know you girls have three month rules."

Melanie laughed. "What?"

"Yeah. I had some female friends before explain it to me that it generally takes three months to see their true colors of the person you're dating."

Melanie laughed knowing there was some general truth to what he was saying.

"Well, we've been talking, dating for three months now. I've shown you my true colors from the beginning. I figured by now you'd know that you do wanna be with me."

Melanie could hear the agitation in Aaron's voice.

She sat up with an unsympathetic look on her face. "Listen here, need I remind you that it was your idea that I date other guys to decide if I really wanted to be with you?"

"Yeah, but I knew with the connection that we have that you'd pick me by now." Aaron blew out a long breath of frustration.

Melanie hated that things couldn't be simpler than they were at the moment. She honestly did care for Aaron and recognized the connection she had with him, but thinking back over the past month with Damon, and how easy it was for them to go somewhere without being judged, she enjoyed Damon for making her life simpler in a way that Aaron wouldn't. Plus, Damon was easy on the eyes and had a lot of the qualities a woman would want in a man. She knew that she wouldn't have had the same experience at the production that night with Aaron as she did with Damon. She didn't have to imagine the responses and stares she would get at a place like that being on Aaron's arm because she had gone through many of those daunting situations with him already.

She knew what she needed to do.

"Look Aaron, there's no need for me to lie and say I don't like you and I don't care about you. I think that's clear from when we're together or on the phone, but I don't wanna live my life always defending who I choose to love and why I choose to love them."

"So what are you saying?" Aaron sat up on his couch hoping Melanie wouldn't say to him what it sounded like she was about to say.

"Aaron, we can't see each other anymore."

"But—"

Melanie hung up the phone. She threw it across the room and balled into a tight form as she cradled a pillow close to her.

21

Karen's plane landed in Chicago. She was coming home after covering a game in Milwaukee with the Bulls.

She took her phone off airplane mode and as it registered her missed calls and texts she saw that she had a voicemail from Kyle. She pressed the button so that she could listen to it.

For as mad as she was that he had practically shut her out of his life for the past month or so, to hear his voice was soothing to her. It comforted her in a way she hadn't been comforted in a while. She knew when he first started pursuing her, now close to two years ago, how hard she would fall for him if she let herself. She fell alright; she knew she had fallen flat on her back for him and that was okay for her as long as he was down there with her, but when he decided to put space between them, that hurt to her core. It was literally like someone had a vice grip around her lungs squeezing and releasing them whenever Kyle came to her mind. She wasn't at her best without him.

She put the phone up to her ear.

"Karen," he paused for a minute. "Hey, it's me, Kyle. I saw you at the game tonight. You looked good as always. If you can, will you stop by tonight when you get back."

Karen pulled the phone away from her ear smiling and crying, thinking his message was over, but when she heard something else, she rewound the message a little and quickly put the phone back up to her ear.

"...get back...I miss you."

He's missed me? She smiled, but then became enraged as thoughts flooded her mind. *Well, if he's missed me, why in the hell hasn't he opened the door when I come over or answer when I call him?* She was confused as she wiped tears from her face. *How can you miss me but not try to see me, Kyle? I don't get why he would pursue me the way he did, win me over, love me the way he did, but then push me away as he has this past month. Hunh? Why, Kyle? Why?* She laughed at herself as she saw how the woman seated next to her looked at her out the corner of her eye. She was certain that with how many times she had gone back and forth between smiling and crying in the past few minutes, the woman must have thought she was bipolar or something.

She wiped her face of the last of her tears and pulled the compact mirror from her purse to freshen her look. She strutted off the plane as it emptied, still battling her inner thoughts. *Lord, help me to listen to him first and hear him out and try not to snap on him as I really want to.* She was glad Kyle had called her to come over to his place. She was determined not to leave him that night until it was clear if they had a future together or not.

***

Karen stood outside of Kyle's condo and took a deep breath. She was ready to knock on the door, but it slowly swung open.

Kyle stood, with no crutches, on the other side of it smiling. He looked at her. Her eyes were red, so he knew she had been crying. He hated that he was probably the reason why, but he planned to fix that. "Come in." He opened the door fully.

His deep, sexy voice warmed her.

"Thank you." She stepped in and closed the door.

She watched him as he slowly limped from the door. He placed his hand on the small of her back and guided her over to a prepared meal in his dining area.

Karen smiled as she looked up to him. "I see you still refuse to use your crutches."

Kyle grinned. "Yeah, but I'm doing much better than the last time I saw you, so the doctor gave me some leeway not to use them all the time."

Karen tilted her head to the side as her tiny nose wrinkled. "Oh really?"

Kyle laughed. "Okay, I lied. I forgot you know sports injuries and healing time, but really it is much better than it was before. Here, let me take your coat."

Kyle helped Karen out of her coat and threw it on the couch nearby.

She raised one eyebrow at him.

"What? It's just a coat."

Karen conceded. He helped her in her seat and then took the one across from her.

Karen looked around and sniffed. "Dim lights, some Jill Scott playing in the background, and the food smells good. I know you didn't cook it." She laughed.

"Whatever, woman. You know I can cook."

Karen was enjoying Kyle's company and everything he had prepared for her, but with how hurt he had made her feel that past month, she needed him to know that.

Kyle could only imagine the wheels spinning in Karen's head. He knew how feisty she could be and with how he had distanced himself from her recently, he knew that maybe some of her trust issues had resurfaced. He hoped tonight would solve everything between them. Well, mostly everything. He grabbed her hand as he looked into her eyes. "Now before you say anything, I'm sorry. I'm sorry for being an idiot and shutting you out when I know all you wanted to do was to be here for me."

Karen couldn't help but to cry as she listened to Kyle.

"Karen, you just don't understand how hard it hit me to be told that I would never play ball again. Yeah, I heard them, but it wasn't until that day that I fell in front of you. I couldn't even walk."

Karen heard the angst in his voice. She knew he was holding back his tears.

"It really hit me that day that I would never play my level of basketball again." Kyle clenched his fists and sniffed. "I mean, I wanted to be in the NBA so bad when I was a little boy and then to have that dream come true for me was amazing in itself. But as you know, every player in the league dreams of winning a title, a championship ring. So I worked hard to improve my skills and condition my body to be taken serious in the league. I knew I was in position to get a ring when the Bulls offered me a deal. Yeah, we didn't win it my first season with them, but I swear, Karen, I swear they're taking it all this year." Kyle looked away from Karen trying to contain his emotions.

Karen got up from her seat. She walked over to Kyle and cupped his chin until his eyes met hers. She wanted to sit on his lap, but she wasn't sure if his leg was strong enough to hold her even though she was petite and he still had his well-defined and muscular frame. "Kyle, I know this has been hard for you, baby, and that's why I was here for you as much as I could be. I was trying to take some of the load off you."

Kyle tried to lower his head again, but Karen kept a firm grip on his face.

"Baby, it's not over for you. You're still a Bull. You get a ring when everyone else on the team gets one this year." She smiled.

"But it won't be the same." He managed to loosen his face from her grip. He scooted his chair back to create space between them. "It won't be the same. Whenever someone looks back at the stats for the year, especially sports heads, they'll say yeah, he got a ring, but he never touched the court majority of the season. It won't be the same. I've gone from being a starter to not even being a bench warmer."

Karen stared quietly at the sudden hopelessness in Kyle. She wanted to console him, but she could sense it was best if she let him talk as much as he needed to.

He let his elbows rest on his knees as he lowered his head into his hands. He rubbed his head vehemently.

Karen cursed herself for staring at his muscles as they flexed while he was grieving. He was so handsome to her. He still sent chills down her spine.

He finally looked up to her. "I'm sorry for putting you out that day. With everything going on with my leg, finding out Mercedes wanted to take Gabby back to Miami, and then you going behind my back talking to her like I couldn't handle my business, it was too much for me. I just needed everyone to get away from me."

Karen moved closer to him. "But Kyle, I wasn't questioning your ability to get the situation with Mercedes under control, I was just trying to help out. I thought maybe if she heard the benefits of letting Gabby stay near you from someone other than you, then she'd be more willing to do so." She wanted to reach out to him but she didn't want him to pull back from her anymore. Her heart could only take so much rejection from him.

Kyle looked into her eyes and saw the nervousness they held. He looked at her petite body almost shaking. He smiled. "Come here." He extended his hand out to her. She placed her hand in his and he pulled her down to sit on his thigh, but Karen hesitated to do so.

He laughed. "It's okay. This leg isn't broke and as long as you don't kick my injured leg, I'll be fine."

She eased down on to his leg as he held her tightly around her waist. He pulled on her chin until their eyes met and he stared into the slanted beauties for a while.

Is it the way, you love me baby... Jill Scott's voice crooned through the speakers and Kyle started singing along with the music to Karen.

Karen started singing, too.

Their faces drew closer and closer to one another until their noses touched. Karen closed her eyes as Kyle's mouth covered hers.

Kyle moaned as he gently gripped the back of Karen's head pulling her closer to him. His tongue searched her mouth as if they had never kissed before. He was eager to reclaim every part of it as his.

He soon pulled back from her knowing there was still something else he needed to say. "I have missed you so much."

"I've missed you, too." Karen gripped his neck wanting to deepen their kiss.

He laughed. "No wait, let me finish." He panted, catching his breath while Karen's chest heaved up and down. *Man, she looks good in this dress.*

"I've missed you and I'm sorry I let my pride get in the way. Instead of pushing you away and hurting you as I can tell I did, I should've just been upfront with you with how I was feeling and better dealt with my anger."

Karen's lips curved into a half smile. "I admit that it hurt, a lot, when you put me out that day, ignored my calls, wouldn't open your door for me." She released one finger from her fist at a time to count the ways in which he hurt her.

Kyle laughed. "Okay, I get it." He kissed each one of her counting fingers.

Karen continued talking, "But as much as I wanted to just wallow, in my heart I also knew that you were dealing with a lot, some heavy stuff. You just better not push me away like that ever again," she punched him in his shoulder, "or there won't be a reunion for us ever again." She punched him in his shoulder again.

"Ahhh." Kyle grimaced.

"What?" Her eyes seemed to bulge from their sockets as she gasped and covered her mouth with both of her hands. "Oh my God, Kyle! Did I hit your leg? I'm so sorry, baby." She sat still not wanting to move at all for fear of hurting him again.

Kyle fell back in his chair laughing.

Karen's eyebrows furrowed. "What?"

"You didn't hurt me. I've honestly been wanting to get somebody like that for the past few weeks." He continued laughing.

Her nostrils flared as she poked her lips out. "You jerk." She pouted and tried to get off him and walk away, but he held her down.

"I'm sorry." He laughed, planting kisses on her neck.

"Nope. You play too much. Get away from me." She pushed at him.

"No, I love you too much to let you go again." He puckered his lips.

She smiled. She stopped struggling with him and looked into his eyes. She saw love in them. She pecked his lips and wrapped her arms around his neck.

"So we're good? You and I?"

"You tell me." She cocked her head at him.

"Yes. We are." He took a deep breath. "But I have some bad news."

Karen raised one eyebrow at him. "What now?"

"Mercedes really is moving back to Miami with Gabby."

"I'm sorry to hear that. I wish you two would've come to some type of agreement where you both get to be around her all the time."

Kyle began to avert eye contact with Karen.

She grabbed his chin forcing his head still so she could look him in the eyes. "What are you not telling me?" With a demanding look on her face, she kept a firm grip on his chin.

He cleared his throat before speaking. "Um, um. I can't lose Gabby, Karen."

"You won't lose her, she'll be just a phone call and a plane ride away."

"Um, honey, sweetie, I don't want that type of relationship with my daughter. I wanna tuck her in at night as often as I can. Take her to her dance classes on Saturday mornings. Drop her off at school during the weekdays. I wanna be, have to be, there for her."

"So what are you saying, Kyle?" Karen's heart began to skip beats waiting for Kyle to speak.

He gently loosened her grip on his chin and lowered his head. He couldn't look her in her eyes as he said, "If Gabby is moving back to Miami, then I am, too."

22

"Well, thank you so much for tonight. I had another great evening with you." Melanie looked over and smiled at Damon.

"Always a pleasure for me to be in your presence." He grabbed her hand and kissed the back of it.

Kissing the back of her hand was no longer cute to her since Aaron wasn't around to do it anymore. He started it anyway.

"Well, let me know when you make it home. I better let you go so the other cars behind you can pull up to the door too." Melanie reached for the door handle but Damon tugged on her arm.

"Melanie, would it be okay if I came up to hang out with you longer? I'm not ready for the night to end."

Melanie paused. Aaron was the last guy she had let up to her condo, but he was no longer in her life. She shook her head knowing she needed to stop comparing Damon to Aaron. She chose Damon over Aaron and she needed to move forward with him uninhibited. She looked over at him. "Sure. Go park and I'll wait in the lobby for you."

Lonnie saw Melanie trying to get out of the car and rushed to hold the door open for her.

"Thanks, Mr. Lonnie." She smiled at him as he closed the car door behind her.

"No problem. How was your evening?" He also held the door of the building open for her.

"It's not over yet. So I'll have to answer that question for you the next time I see you." She followed him to the desk he worked from.

"Not over yet?"

"Yeah. My date, Damon, went to park his car. We're gonna hang out a while longer tonight."

"Oh."

Melanie noted the cynicism in his voice. "Why'd you say 'oh' like that?" She leaned in over the desk.

"No reason. No reason at all." He fumbled through some papers.

"You're always full of wisdom. You never say something just to be talking. You can be honest with me. Why'd you say 'oh' like that?"

"Well, Ms. Melanie, if you want me to be honest, then that's what I'll be. I don't like that guy you got out of the car with."

"You've never even met him. How do you know you don't like him?"

"I may not have met him as in you formally introducing him to me, but I've met him alright. I've met his kind."

Melanie's eyebrows furrowed. "I'm not following you, Mr. Lonnie. Just spit it out."

"I've been here sometimes when he's dropped you off. He's never made eye contact with me."

"Maybe he never saw you."

"Oh he's seen me alright, but he refuses to make eye contact with me. I told you before, I can't trust a man that won't look me in the eyes. Now that other guy that used to be around here with you, that white guy."

Melanie pouted.

"He was a keeper."

"But you didn't really know him either." Melanie shook her head.

"I knew him well enough to know he was a good and honest man from the way he looked me right in my eyes and gave me a firm handshakes each time I saw him."

"Not all men are the same."

"You're right, because if they're not a man, then they're still a boy."

Damon walked through the glass doors.

Lonnie looked up first. "Here he comes. Let's see who's right."

Melanie turned to watch Damon come towards them. He kept his eyes on Melanie as he made his way to the desk. He put his arm around her when he reached her.

She looked over to him. "Damon this is Mr. Lonnie, Mr. Lonnie this is Damon."

Damon looked in Lonnie's direction. "What's up, Lonnie?"

Melanie furrowed her eyebrows but remained silent. *I called him Mr. Lonnie, but Damon referred to him as just Lonnie.*

"Hello young man. How are you?" Lonnie looked at Damon and held his hand out waiting for Damon to make eye contact with him and shake his hand. Lonnie tightened his lips at the limp handshake Damon gave him. It left so much more to be desired of a man for Melanie.

Melanie stared between the two of them hoping that she wouldn't see what Lonnie had said to her earlier. Her shoulders slumped when she saw that Damon never made full eye contact with Lonnie and she could clearly see the fragility in the handshake he shared with Lonnie.

"Well, see you later, Mr. Lonnie." Melanie gave him a half smile.

"I'll see you soon enough, Ms. Melanie, and remember what we talked about." Lonnie went back to reading the newspaper as he shook his head.

"What was that all about?" Damon asked Melanie as they stood at the elevators waiting for it to arrive to the lobby floor.

"Oh nothing."

Damon looked back and saw Lonnie was staring at him with a look of pity. He quickly turned his attention back to Melanie. "I don't like him."

Melanie turned to Damon with her face scrunched up. "Why not? You don't even know him. Mr. Lonnie is a great, caring man." She looked past Damon to see Lonnie staring at them. She waved at him as they entered the elevator.

"I just don't." Damon stepped in and leaned against the back wall of the elevator.

The door closed and Melanie shielded the keypad with her body as she entered her code to take them to her floor.

"Don't worry, I won't try to sneak up on you just yet." Damon smirked as he tickled Melanie's waist.

She laughed and fidgeted trying to escape his grasp.

"You better not. And please stop. I'm really ticklish."

"Aha. Now I know superwoman's kryptonite." He laughed and reached out to her again, but she escaped his grasp once more.

The elevator doors opened and Melanie rushed out heading to her door as Damon was adamant on tickling her.

He caught up to her at her front door. She held her arm out to keep him at bay. "I don't know why you think I'm superwoman."

"You're a strong, black woman, educated, talented, health conscious, socially aware, and so much more. You're definitely a superwoman. Just let me be your superman." He stared into her eyes as he slowly walked towards her. He lowered her arm she held out and pulled it around his waist as he drew closer to her. He towered her as he lowered his face within an inch of hers and stared into her eyes as he pulled her even closer to him. He searched her eyes for permission to kiss her and when he thought he saw the answer he wanted, his lips met hers for a brief second before she turned away from him and the full force of what he wanted to be a passionate kiss with her landed on her cheek.

One side of her mouth curled up in uncertainty. "Let's just go inside."

He lifted off her allowing her to turn to face the door.

She put her key in the lock, twisted it, and opened the door. She hit the lights and he walked in behind her. "Lock the door please."

"Okay." Damon stared at her with his eyebrows raised as he secured all the locks on her door.

She took her coat off and hung it on the rack and then waited for him to do the same.

"Melanie, is everything okay? I mean out in the hallway I thought you wanted to kiss me, but I went in to do it and you turned away."

"I'm sorry." She hung his coat on the rack.

"No, I'm sorry if I'm rushing you. It's just that I like you and I've really wanted to kiss you since the first day I met you."

"Thanks." Melanie gave him a half smile.

He gave her a slow, disbelieving shake of the head. "Thanks?"

She feigned indifference to his response as she shrugged her shoulders and headed towards her kitchen. "You want something to drink?"

"Sure." He followed her and sat on a stool at the island.

"What would you like?"

"It doesn't matter. You pick, but back to that 'thanks'."

Melanie grabbed two wine glasses and a bottle of red wine. She turned to face Damon. "I didn't know what else to say at the time. I mean you're right, I did want to kiss you, but then at the same time, something inside of me was screaming it might be too soon for that."

Damon slumped his shoulders. "It's cool. No rush. When you're ready, I'm sure you'll plant those soft, plump lips of yours on mine." He winked at her.

"Hey, stop staring at my lips." Melanie pretended to be appalled as she handed him his glass of wine. "Come on, let's go over to the couch."

Damon followed her to the couch. She extended her hand out for him to have a seat and then she headed to her stereo system. She turned on one of her favorite artist, Lianne La Havas. Smooth mid-tempo guitar strings and piano keys filled the room. Melanie smiled, adjusting the volume. "Ever heard her—" Melanie turned to speak to Damon, but unbeknownst to her, he was right behind her. She bumped into him causing the red wine they each held to spill and soak both of their shirts.

"I'm so sorry, I didn't mean to startle you. I was about to tell you I was right behind you when you turned around."

Melanie looked down at her stained sweater dress and then at his stained button-up. "It's okay, but if you'll excuse me, I need to get out of this. It's starting to stick to me and it's my favorite." Melanie pouted. "I wanna try and salvage it. I'll be back as soon as I can." Melanie rushed off to the bathroom in her room.

Damon still stood near the stereo system trying to figure out what he would do until Melanie returned. His shirt was stained, too. He unbuttoned his baby blue shirt to see that the white undershirt he had on was stained as well and was now sticking to him. He took both of them off.

After laying his shirts down flat on the back of the couch nearby, he looked down to see a puddle of wine on the floor. He went to the kitchen and grabbed paper towels to clean up the spill. When he cleaned it up the floor was still sticky so he went back to the kitchen to get water to aid in cleaning up the mess.

The doorbell rang.

He looked to the door, but since it wasn't his home he wouldn't open it.

It rang again.

"Melanie, someone is at your door." Damon yelled in the direction of her room.

"It's just my best friend. She has a key. She can let herself in."

The doorbell rang again.

Damon looked down at his shirtless body and then mumbled to himself, "Oh well, I guess her best friend will get an eye full, too."

The doorbell rang again.

"Melanie, I locked all of the locks. I don't think she can get in with just a key," he yelled over the music.

"Okay. Well, open it for me please. I'll be out in a minute." Damon quickly threw away the paper towels and rushed to the door to stop her best friend from ringing it one more time.

He opened the door.

"Damon!" Aaron yelled.

Damon smirked.

"What are you doing here and with no shirt on?" Aaron asked, confusion written all over his face.

"I'm here with my girl. What are you doing here?"

"Your girl? Your girl! This is Melanie's place. My Melanie, so I know your girl doesn't live here."

"She's not your Melanie. Remember she couldn't deal with you being white. She needs a strong, black man like me." Damon slapped his naked chest.

"Man, get out of the way. Melanie! Melanie!" Aaron tried to bombard his way past Damon but Damon shoved him back forcefully into the hallway.

Melanie came running out of her room.

"What is going on out here?" She rushed towards the front door. She paused for a moment looking at Damon's chiseled body. *Jeesh, I knew he was muscular, but not like that. Damn!*

Her fantasies of Damon's body lying next to hers was interrupted when she saw Damon and Aaron tussling.

"Stop it! Stop it!" She screamed to the top of her lungs.

Aaron stopped, hearing the alarm in her voice, but Damon continued trying to wrestle with Aaron.

Aaron broke free from Damon and rushed over to Melanie. "Melanie, what is he doing here? With no shirt on?"

"What do you mean what is he doing here? I'm dating him now. What are you doing here?" Melanie huffed.

"Yeah, what are you doing here, and how'd you get up here anyway?" Damon pushed Aaron.

"Yeah, how did you?" Melanie eyebrows raised. Her nostrils flared.

"Shut up talking to me." Aaron pushed Damon back.

"Enough!" Melanie screamed. "Damon, you go over there. Aaron you stay right here." She pointed to a spot next to her.

Damon frowned. He wanted to be next to her.

Melanie turned her anger to Aaron first.

"What are you doing here?"

Aaron was red with frustration and desperation laced his voice as he said, "Melanie, you haven't been answering any of my calls or responding to any of my messages. I know you said you couldn't be with me anymore, but I just can't accept that. You and I deserve a chance." He gripped and pulled curls on his head. "Man, I should've never listened to you." He clenched his teeth.

"Genius, right?" Damon said, smirking.

Melanie looked between the two of them. "Shut up!" Her shaky high pitched voice bellowed throughout her condo. "And how do you two know each other?"

"He's my best friend, or at least I thought he was." Aaron charged at Damon but Melanie's outstretched arm stopped him from doing so. He could have easily went past her, but wanting to respect her, he stayed back.

"Yeah, you thought." Damon's muscles flexed.

"You knew how much I cared for her, man. Hell, you came up with the idea to get her to see I was the one for her." Aaron's voice was filled with pain.

Damon laughed.

"What?" Melanie was confused.

"Man, you've always gotten the black girls I wanted. One whiff of vanilla chocolate and they were putty in your hand." Damon shook his head walking towards Aaron.

Aaron frowned. "What?"

"You thought because you hung around me and my family since we were kids that you were one of us, that you really were black."

"Where is all of this coming from?" Aaron's forehead creased with deep lines.

Melanie was too shocked to speak.

"Oh it's been there for a long time. See I dealt with it when it was the chicks in high school and college. I wasn't ready to settle down then, but now that I'm ready to start a family you just had to pick the one I wanted. I saw her first." Damon stood nose to nose with Aaron.

Melanie slid in between the two of them. "What?" She threw her hands up in the air before propping them at her waist.

Aaron backed up creating lots of space between him and Melanie. He didn't want her to get caught in between him and Damon if they fought. He hoped that Damon would at least have enough sense to either move her out of the way or run around her to fight him.

Melanie stood flat-footed in front of Damon. She looked up staring into his eyes demanding him to answer her.

He looked into hers and hastened his response. "I saw you first. One day at a race, I was standing outside of the corral waiting for him to show up. I was admiring you, but I also kept looking around for him. Just when I had made up my mind to step to you, I look up to see you two talking and laughing. It pissed me off." Damon turned and punched the nearby wall. "I wanted you, but you seemed to want him. That day, I decided that I would get you no matter what."

Melanie was enraged. Fury overtook her and she slapped Damon. "So what am I? A door prize?"

Damon rubbed his jaw tasting the blood in his mouth. "I deserved that."

"And so much more." Melanie spewed at him.

She turned to face Aaron. "So was this a game between you two? See who could make me fall the hardest, the fastest for them?"

"No, Melanie." Aaron moved towards her, but she stared him down, balling up her fist.

He didn't want to receive the same blow that Damon did so he stayed back. "Melanie, this was never a game to me. I saw you at a race way before the day I spoke to you and I wanted you from that day, I just never said anything to you. I swear I didn't know this fool was dating you." Aaron clenched his teeth as he stared at Damon.

Damon laughed. "I was smarter than you this time around. I wasn't gonna let you get the girl of my dreams. I took note of everything you told me about her so that when we were together I could make her see I was the one for her."

Melanie shook her head. She held up her finger silencing the brewing tit for tat between Aaron and Damon. She turned her attention to Damon. "So we had so much in common because Aaron was spoon feeding you details of my life?"

Damon wasn't so quick to respond to Melanie. He saw the hurt mixed with anger in her eyes. He really did like her. "Melanie, yes I knew what you liked before you ever told me some stuff, but I swear we really do have a lot in common. You can't be you with him. The black you. The kinky haired you. You can't have black love with him."

Melanie threw her hands up in disgust. Her nostrils flared as she turned to face Aaron.

"Melanie, I swear I didn't know he was dating you," Aaron said before she could even question him.

"I can't trust either of you." She continued to look at Aaron. "You're the one that suggested I date other guys, so how do I really know if you all weren't playing some sick joke on me?"

"Look into my eyes and tell me if you think I was playing a joke on you."

Melanie's eyes watered with frustration and confusion as she looked into Aaron's. She thought she saw sincerity in them, but with the emotional roller coaster she had been on the past year, she didn't know if she could trust her judgment at all. "Please leave," She said, low.

"Melanie, if you give me another chance I swear I'll show you I'm the one for you." Damon circled in front of Melanie to speak to her.

"Damon. Get your shit and get out now."

Damon's eyes widened seeing the dead stare in Melanie's eyes. He didn't even know she had it in her to curse. He grabbed his stuff and headed to the door. He stopped in the doorway looking back at Aaron as if to say *you better be leaving, too.*

Aaron walked closer to Melanie. "Can we talk about this?"

She slowly looked up at him. The softness in his voice was tearing at her heart, but he couldn't be trusted; her judgment couldn't be trusted. She finally made eye contact with him. "Leave now." A tear escaped her eye.

Aaron didn't want to hurt her any more than the pain he saw in her eyes. He turned and walked out the door violently brushing past Damon.

Damon closed the door after he and Aaron walked out.

Melanie screamed. Nothing made sense to her. She looked over her shoulder to see the wine glasses on the island. She rushed to grab them and threw them as hard as she could at the front door.

She continued to scream out in frustration as she ran to her room to find comfort in her bed under the covers.

23

Kyle sat with his feet propped up on his ottoman. He was watching footage from the last Bulls game. "Damn! They look good without me, but they would be so much better if I were able to play."

Karen came out of the kitchen. She handed him a plate of food.

He smiled at her. "You know I can move around on my own, don't you?"

"I know, but I thought it would be selfish of me all up in your house cooking me something to eat and I not give you any." She sat down in the big chair across from him. "I heard you. They do look good out there, but they would definitely look better with you starting. So are you going to the game tonight? It's the last game of the regular season." Her eyebrows lifted as she bit into a fry. It had been months since his fall. He finally seemed to come out of his depression after finding out he would never play again. She was proud of him traveling with the team for some of their away games as well as attending pretty much all of the home games. His

239

teammates were very supportive of him, even working out with him to help his recovery. They pushed him to do more every day.

He put his plate down on the side of him, wiped his hands of salt, and stared at Karen. "I hate sometimes that you know so much about basketball." He laughed.

"What?" She frowned.

"Because, I can't get over on you with excuses."

"You sure can't, but why would you want to?"

"With any other woman, I could tell her my leg is hurting or something and she wouldn't bother me about tonight, but you, you've seen my most recent cat-scans and MRIs. You see the progress I've made with recovering, but still know I won't ever be the same again. You won't let me wallow in pity. You've pushed me to better instead of bitter. I thank you for that."

"My pleasure." Karen winked at him and bit into her chicken sandwich.

Kyle turned the TV off, got off the couch, and limped over to her. He sat on the ottoman across from her.

"What? Why are you looking at me like that?"

"Because you're beautiful."

Karen ignored him and grabbed her chicken sandwich again.

"You're beautiful. I know last year you almost married that jerk, but you accepted me instead. I had so much planned for us this year, but with my injury and Mercedes taking Gabby back to Miami, things didn't work out the way I planned them too."

"It's okay, Kyle. We're still together, and you'll get your ring this year with the Bulls. Shoot, even coach Hoiberg said he'd let you suit up and get on the floor a game during each round of the playoffs. You will still get your dream, a ring, even after all you've been through." She dipped her fries in BBQ sauce and bit into them.

He smiled and moved closer to her. "Yeah, well, when this season started, my plan wasn't just to get a ring, it was to give you a ring, too, by now."

Karen's eyebrows furrowed. "Hunh?"

"Karen, since nothing has turned out the way I wanted it to this year, I might as well do this now and here, from my heart."

"Kyle, what are you talking about?" She took another bite out of her sandwich.

He lowered himself from the ottoman to one knee. He laughed seeing Karen was oblivious to his motions as she focused on her food. He reached into his pocket and grabbed what he needed to complete his mission.

"Karen? Karen Shanice Roberts?"

"Hunh?" She didn't look up at him from her plate, but instead looked over at her vibrating phone.

"I've loved you since the first time I laid my eyes on you. Through everything these past two years, you've been there for me and have shown me what true love is. I'm honored to know you."

"I love you, too, Kyle." She continued to look at her twitter page responding to fans comments.

He laughed thinking that maybe the sparkle from the six carat princess cut diamond engagement ring he held in front of her wasn't big enough to draw her attention. "Karen, would you do me the honor of being my wife?" He held the ring out closer to her waiting for her to finally look up at him and it.

"Hunh?" She continued tweeting on her phone.

He cleared his throat and talked louder than before, "I said, Karen Shanice Roberts, will you please pay attention to me and accept my proposal for you to make me the happiest man on earth and become my wife?"

Karen lifted her head from her phone. She saw Kyle on one knee. She saw the gorgeous princess cut ring he held in his hand. She looked back at him and saw such intense admiration for her in his eyes. Her brain finally started to register what was happening right in front of her. She dropped her phone. She took the plate from her lap and placed it on the arm of the chair. She scooted closer to the edge of her seat as she lifted her hands and covered her mouth in astonishment when what Kyle asked her finally sunk in. She shrieked.

"What? Don't act surprised like I never was gonna do this. It hasn't been the topic of discussion in a while, but you know this is what I've always wanted with you. I thought you did, too. So will you say yes?" Kyle's eyebrows raised as he held in his breath.

"Yes. Yes. Yes!" Karen repeated her proclamation as she moved in closer to Kyle and gripped his face, pulling him close to her. She kissed him passionately.

He laughed as he pushed her back some and pulled her down on his knee, but she wouldn't lower herself on it.

"Kyle, I can't sit on your knee. It's the leg you hurt." Her eyes bulged and compassion gripped her voice.

"Don't worry. I got you." He gently lowered her onto his knee. "See, I'm fine."

She twisted her mouth. "I guess."

"So, you're going to be my wife and move to Miami with me?" He smiled and planted a kiss on her lips.

Karen jumped up and away from Kyle. "Miami? Kyle, I can't move to Miami. My job, my life is here." She pointed to the ground where she stood.

Kyle slowly stood to his feet and flexed his injured leg. "Karen, you fly across the country to broadcast away games all the time. Living in Miami shouldn't make that much of a difference in your schedule." He put his large hands up to his waist causing his oversized shirt to cling to his waist and highlight his long, muscular legs.

Karen stared at them and lost thought of what she was going to say for a moment. "It is too a major difference. What kind of wife could I be to you if I'm never at home?"

Kyle let out a deep sigh. He threw his hands up to his head and interlaced them behind his head. Karen's response wasn't the one he expected. Granted he didn't propose to her in the fanciest way, but after her fiasco with Dennis, he knew she was more concerned with her life after a proposal and wedding than anything else. He thought she wanted that life with him.

"And have you forgotten about my weekly show? I tape that here in the Chi." Karen turned her back to Kyle to laugh.

"So what are you saying, Karen? You won't marry me?" Kyle's eyebrows met each other in the center of his forehead. His jaws tightened.

She smeared a frown on her face before she turned back to face him. "Kyle, you knew of my career ambitions since the day we met. I just can't leave everything behind that I've worked so hard for."

"So, I guess that's a no." Kyle turned and quickly limped to the front door. He snatched his keys from a stand nearby and grabbed the doorknob.

"Kyle, wait," Karen yelled out.

Kyle took a deep breath before slowly looking over his shoulder at her. "What, Karen?"

There was too much anger and hurt in his voice for her to go on. She knew it was time to come clean to him. She slowly walked over to him smiling.

He completely turned to face her. "Why are you smiling? Do you think this is funny? I thought we would be together, get married, but now I find out we never will. I don't find that funny. I love you." He turned to pull the door open.

Karen pulled on his hand and interlaced hers with his.

Kyle looked at their hands together. *How is it that the woman I love so much doesn't wanna marry me?* He kept his head low staring at their hands still intertwined. *But you're leaving her, Kyle.* His conscious reminded him.

He looked back at her still smiling. He was confused with her jovial mood when he was in so much pain knowing that they wouldn't be together anymore. He leaned down and kissed the top of her head. "Bye, Karen."

He turned to walk out the door, but she pulled him back yet again. "But, Kyle, this is your place." She looked up at him trying to contain her laughter.

"I don't know why you're so happy, and I do know it's my place. I need to get some air. I'll stay gone long enough for you to pack your things you have here."

He turned to open the door once more, but Karen jumped in front of him before he could do so. "Kyle." She laughed.

He stepped back from her. "I don't get you right now. What's so funny? It's starting to piss me off."

Karen gripped her stomach laughing even harder than she did before.

"Karen, just let me leave and you can laugh here alone all you want to." He walked towards the door, but she held her arms up to stop him.

"I can't let you leave. I have something to tell you." She wiped tears from her eyes after laughing so hard. She didn't know she would get such a kick out of what she was doing. She hadn't planned to tell him like this, but his proposal to her kind of made it easy to joke with him. She knew the joke was over though. She could see he really was hurting. "Kyle, I had no idea you would propose to me today. I had already planned to tell you something. Sorry for joking with you for so long just now, but—"

"But what, Karen? I wanna laugh too, because right now, ain't shit funny to me."

"Hey. Watch your mouth." Karen pouted.

"Sorry," he mumbled.

She put her arms around his waist and looked up into his eyes as best as she could. The difference in their heights was really putting a strain on her neck.

He didn't return her embrace. He kept his arms to his side bracing himself for whatever else she had to say.

"Kyle, yes the life I've built up to this point has been based out of Chicago, and I understand you feel the need to go to Miami to raise your daughter. I admire you for that. I'm willing to travel as much as needed to keep broadcasting for the Bulls, that is at least until we start having kids of our own."

Kyle smiled and kissed the tip of her nose, but then frowned. "Well, what about your show here? I don't want you to look back years from now regretting anything." He wrapped his arms around her.

"I won't. I talked to my bosses about three months ago and told them about my desire to relocate to Miami. At first they said I couldn't tape there because they didn't have any studio space to produce my show there, but now that they have merged with a major network there, I can tape there and broadcast to an even wider market. Instead of just being national, Kyle I'm about to be international and yes I'll marry you." She squealed.

He picked her up off her feet and spun her around in circles before he finally felt a strain on his leg. "Ouch."

"What, baby?" She jumped out of his arms staring at him. "See you're doing too much."

She wrapped her arm around his waist and tried to usher him over to the couch as if her small frame could support his substantially larger one.

His limp was more pronounced than what it was earlier as they made it over to the couch and she helped him to sit down.

He laughed. "I'm not helpless, Karen."

"I know." She helped him lift his leg onto the couch. She tried to walk away but he pulled her down on top of him.

"Kyle, stop. I don't want to hurt your leg."

"You won't. It's down there and you're up here." He smiled. "Woman, your petite body doesn't span the length of mine."

"So." She rolled her eyes.

"So, I love you and I'm glad you're mine." He kissed her lips, but then pulled back from her. "Hey, were you really gonna move with me to Miami even though we aren't married yet?"

She smiled. "Nope, actually I wasn't."

His eyebrows furrowed and he cocked his head at her.

She laughed. "You've been pretty much back to your old self lately. I knew the Kyle who wanted to marry me was still in there, I figured he would ask me soon enough."

He pecked her on her lips. "So, do you still want a big wedding?"

"No, I just want you."

24

"Thanks for meeting me here and agreeing to talk to her with me." Andrew smiled at Melanie as they stood in the driveway outside of Marie's house.

"I'm not sure she'll give you any answers, but we can at least try." Melanie shrugged her shoulders trying to appear hopeful in front of him.

"Thanks again. I see you really are coming around to me." Andrew gave her a half smile.

"Whatever." She pressed her lips tight together. "But yeah, I don't gag and get so weirded out anymore when it comes to mind that you're my brother."

Andrew stopped in the walkway waiting to see if Melanie would indeed shiver like she normally did whenever he was around and someone mentioned they were brother and sister. When he saw no trace of her body responding to him in disgust, he said again, "I see. And it only took about a year."

"Some things take longer than others."

"Yup."

They made it to the front door and rang the doorbell.

"Why don't you use your key?" Andrew asked.

"Well, after you told me about my dad being over here that time, I stopped by another time unannounced. You know my mom…" She looked at Andrew's pleading face. "Our mom doesn't work and is not a part of any activities that keep her busy during the day, or at least I thought." Melanie rang the doorbell again and continued telling Andrew the story. "Well, I let myself in, but she was nowhere in sight as I called out to her. I finally made it upstairs in my search. When I got to her bedroom I heard moans and groans coming from it that had me thinking maybe she was in bed watching TV. Well, I was wrong." Melanie shivered in disgust as her face contorted showing her disdain for whatever she was thinking about.

"What?" Andrew waited anxiously for Melanie to answer his question.

"I opened the door without knocking and caught them, you know…"

"Doing what?" Andrew snickered.

"Why are you trying to make me relive that moment?" Melanie shivered in disgust again as Andrew laughed uncontrollably. "Yeah, laugh at my pain."

Melanie knocked on the door.

"You think she's at home?" Andrew asked.

"Yup, and so is my dad."

"Hunh? How do you know he's here?"

"For one, that's his SUV in the driveway."

Andrew looked back at the black Arcadia.

"And for two, they didn't tell many people yet, but they went to the courthouse and got remarried a week after you caught him here."

Andrew's eyes widened. "Wow."

"I know, right?"

"So, how do you feel about that?"

"I think it's great. Now my dad gets to experience the woman he saw trapped inside of my mother when they were together. She's much happier and lively, except when it comes to you asking about your dad."

Someone could be heard moving things on the inside.

"I hate to put her through this. I wish the past didn't happen to her the way it did, but just like I wouldn't have rested until I found out who my birth mother is, learning how I came to be still hasn't changed my mind about wanting to know who my birth father is."

The door opened and Marie smiled, panting out of breath. "Oh, both of my children here, now, together. Come in." She ushered them in. "Why didn't you all call before you came over?"

Melanie hugged and kissed her mother first and then Andrew followed suit.

"Because you've been avoiding us when we try to talk to you together," Melanie said as she stepped completely into the house. "Where's Dad?"

"Oh, he's upstairs." Marie smiled clearing her throat.

"Why the look on your face?" Andrew asked Melanie as they rounded the couch to sit down.

She leaned in to him and with a suspicious tone said. "You've been over here enough to know that this living room isn't normally arranged like this, right?"

Marie came over and sat in the arm chair near them. "Oh fix your face. I heard you. This is my house and I can rearrange it anyway I like."

Melanie scanned the room. "But Mom there's no apparent reason for why you have things so out of place, or in their new place as you say."

"Oh shoot, your father and I are grown, this is our house, and we needed to move some things around for our role playing."

Melanie covered her ears and eyes at the same time. "Ma, eww. Too much information for me. You're so liberated now. You wouldn't dare talk like that when I was younger."

"Well, like you said, I'm liberated now."

"Good, so I need you to liberally share who my father is," Andrew said.

Howard made his way down the stairs. He kissed Melanie on her cheek, shook Andrew's hand, and winked at Marie all before heading into the kitchen.

Marie crossed her legs at her knees and began to wring her hands together roughly.

Melanie stood up from the couch and went to her mother's side to comfort and calm her before the manic episode she was sure to come.

"No, it's okay, Melanie. I'm fine, I'm coming to better terms with what happened to me since I told

Andrew how he was conceived. I promised myself and Howard that before I said 'I do' to him again, I would make sure I was emotionally ready to be a good wife to him this time. I made my peace with my past before I said I do, so I'm fine. I can't let it weigh me down anymore."

"So then, you'll tell me?" Andrew stared into her eyes.

She sighed as she looked to Andrew. "It's not me I'm worried about, it's you. I don't think you'll be fine if I tell you who your father is."

Andrew scooted to the end of the couch to draw closer to Marie.

Melanie stood up from the arm of her mother's chair and went and sat on the coffee table in front of Marie. Melanie tried to speak, but Andrew cut her off. "Why won't I be fine? Is it someone I've met before? Someone I know?"

Marie reached out and grabbed Andrew's hands. She looked deep into his eyes. She rubbed his face gently, hoping he would take heed to what she was saying. "Trust me, baby, you don't wanna know."

"But Ma," he squeezed her hand, "I have to know. It's been a burning desire of mine to know my birth father. I remembered you, I just didn't know who you were or where you were. I thank God we reconnected, but I need to know the other half of who made me. I'm sorry if it's insensitive to you."

Marie breathed a deep sigh. She lowered her head and shook it. She looked back up at Andrew. "Baby, if I tell you, there's no going back."

"I know, Ma."

"You're headstrong just like I used to be before it happened to me, so I imagine you'll keep hounding me about it until I tell you." Marie took another deep breath trying to ready herself to tell Andrew the truth.

Andrew smiled warily. "Yup."

"You ever noticed that you look a lot like your adoptive father?" Marie asked. She planned to give out hints and ease Andrew into the knowledge of who his birth father is.

"Yeah, but I just figured that since he had me for so long, we started to look alike. But what does that have to do with you telling me who my birth father is?"

"Drew." She rubbed his face hoping her touch would soften the blow she was soon to deal him. "You are the spitting image of your birth father."

Melanie's eyebrows furrowed. "Ma, if you're gonna tell him, would you tell him already? You keep dancing in circles referencing his adoptive father, but he wants to know who his birth father is."

Tears fell from Marie's eyes.

"Ma, I don't want you to cry. I don't want you to be sad." Andrew caressed the back of Marie's hands as he continued to hold them.

"Drew, I'm not crying for me, I'm crying for you."

"Ma, would you please just give me his name? I'll go look him up on my own and never bother you about it again."

Marie shook her head. "Drew, his name is… his name is Charles Dodson."

Melanie sat up attentively. That name sounded familiar to her.

Andrew's eyebrows furrowed. He was silent for a moment and then he laughed. "That's my adoptive father's name, too."

Marie sat as still as possible studying Andrew's face. She hoped what she told him would sink in already and she wouldn't have to say anymore.

The longer they all sat there quietly, the more pensive Andrew's face became. Moments passed before Andrew started shaking his head and looked up at Marie. "It's just a coincidence they have the same name, right? You aren't really saying that the man who raised me, the one I already call Dad, is the same man who raped you? That's not what you're saying, right? My dad really is my dad?" He looked into Marie's eyes hoping to see denial and that she would confirm with words that he was wrong, but when he looked into them all he saw was a yes.

Melanie sat by, not sure how Andrew would react. She looked from her mother to her brother waiting for someone to say something, do something.

Howard reentered the room. He saw the distressed look on Andrew's face. "What's going on? Is everything okay?"

Andrew looked up confused, hurt, and in disbelief. He shook his head and looked to Marie. "This can't be true. This is just a coincidence. My dad, the loving man that raised me is not the same man that raped you. Nope, you're just confused."

Andrew jumped from the couch and began pacing the floor.

Marie stood and walked over to him. "Drew." She grabbed his arm. "Why do you think I reacted the way I did when I saw that picture of him and your niece that day?"

Andrew thought for a minute. "I don't know, maybe the two men really just look alike, but my dad didn't do what you said he did to you." He tried to walk away from her, but she reached out and grabbed his arm and held him in place in front of her.

"Baby, I'm not confused or wrong. That man in the picture you showed me is the man that raped me." Marie refused to allow tears to escape her eyes as she mentioned being raped again. She was tired of crying over it.

Andrew shook his head again in denial.

"Drew. I didn't just meet your father once."

Andrew's eyebrows furrowed.

Melanie stood up and came closer to them never having heard the story before either.

"He was an adjunct professor for my U.S. History class. He always managed to keep me after class wanting to review an assignment I had turned in. At first he flirted with me subtly and I ignored his advances, but then one day he had me to stay after class and he came right out with telling me how much he wanted me. I felt uncomfortable with where things seemed to be headed and I tried to leave but he blocked me in the room and chased me around until he captured me."

"Ma, why didn't anyone come to help you?" Melanie rubbed her mother's back. "Didn't you scream? Cry out for help?"

"I did at first, before I went numb while he was raping me. After he finished having his way with me, he laid on top of me saying he knew I would be good. He could tell I was a virgin and wanted me since the first day he saw me in class. He said if I would've went along with his flirting and gave him a chance, he wouldn't have had to do what he did, but since I resisted him, he had to have me one way or another."

Andrew stood silent. He seemed to hold his breath.

Howard came over and guided Marie back to the chair she sat in. He sat down next to her.

Melanie went back to her seat on the coffee table in front of Marie.

"Drew, say something." Marie called out to him.

He remained quiet by the mantle over the fireplace looking at the tattered baby picture of him she put up since he had come back into her life.

"Ma, did you ever tell anyone?" Compassion laced Melanie's voice as she leaned forward and rubbed her mother's hands.

"No. I left the room after he did what he did to see that pretty much everyone was gone off campus for a holiday. I rushed back to my room, packed my things, and caught a bus home. I never went back to school. I never told my parents or sisters and brother what happened to me. I pretended to still be in school so my family wouldn't question what had become of me, but I secured public housing and assistance and stayed to myself until I met your father."

"Oh, I'm sorry you had to endure that, Ma. I never knew why you didn't finish college."

Andrew returned to sit on the couch.

"Drew, say something, baby." Marie grabbed his hand.

He shook his head. "I just can't believe that the man that raised me could do something like that to you, to any woman for that matter. He's strict but he's loving. He's kind and mild mannered. He's a great guy and I love him. I'm sorry, but I don' believe it." Andrew got up dazed and walked out leaving the door wide open behind him.

25

Melanie sat in her bed with her laptop on deciding what races she would sign up for.

It had been two weeks since Marie had told Andrew who his father was and Marie and Melanie hadn't heard from him since then. They called and texted him, but it seemed as if his phone had been turned off. Melanie had gone by his house to check on him, but he never came to the door. She had even used her old key she had to his place and she walked in to find that all of his clothes and furniture were still there, but there was no sign of him.

Kyle had been reaching out to find him but his leads to where Andrew might be always turned up empty.

The only other people Melanie knew of that might know where he was and if he was okay were his adoptive parents, but with the knowledge of what his father had did to her mother, she dared not set foot in their house ever again.

She laid back on her pillow and realized that another year had gone by and she still didn't have a happy ending or at least a beautiful beginning as far as love was concerned. *I met Aaron though.* She smiled. *And even though I had a major issue with his race and not wanting to deal with the discrimination that comes along with interracial dating, my hesitation with him was equally driven by my fear of trusting myself to make the best decisions when it comes to my love life. I mean after all, I chose Damon and look where that got me—played.* She looked at her Facebook messages blinking on her screen. She clicked on it to see that she had a new message from Aaron. She had stopped reading them about a month ago. They all said the same thing: He was sorry. He didn't know about Damon. He still wants her in his life, he believes she's the one for him and to give him another chance. *Boy is he persistent.* She smiled as she looked up at the bouquet of flowers on her dresser. It was the most recent one Aaron had sent her. He had sent her something daily since the last time she saw him, when she put him out of her condo. *I'm not reading it.* "Ugh!" She screamed out loud as she hit her bed with both hands. "Why can't I just meet the right one!"

She went online and looked in her log of races she had participated in the year before and signed up for the first three listed in her archives. The first one was the next day. "Good, I need to run to get away from myself." She laughed at herself for thinking that was even possible.

She wished Karen could run with her the next day but with the NBA season being over, Karen had already started taping her new show in Miami. She hated that her best friend decided to just up and leave her like that, but she knew how much Karen and Kyle loved each other, plus her career goals were being met in Miami, too. She smiled thinking how Kyle finally got the ring he wanted when the Bulls became the 2016 NBA champions. She became happier thinking about how Karen would officially become Mrs. Irving at Karen and Kyle's destination wedding in Aruba the next month. She couldn't wait to see her best friend again days before the ceremony. They planned to meet up in Miami and hang out before they headed to the island. *I wonder if Andrew will show up to the wedding. He is the best man.*

And then there's my mom. She's had the best year of her life—reconnecting with her son, beginning to heal from her rape, remarrying my dad, getting out of the house more, and even enrolling back in school to finish her degree. Melanie smiled and a tear trickled down her face. *I'm so happy for her. I guess if I can't experience the happiness I want just yet, I can relish in my mom's and my best friend's.*

She got up from her bed and decided she would go down to her gallery and paint.

***

Melanie stood in the same corral she did at the race last year. She stretched and bobbed her head to the music blaring in her headphones. She was grateful for the visor she wore that shielded her eyes from the bright sun beaming down on her. She shook her head at herself as she looked around possibly hoping to see Aaron. When she didn't, she turned her attention back to the start sign and frowned.

She continued stretching and vibing to her music when she felt a tap on her shoulder. She smiled readying herself to look into Aaron's eyes when she turned to see that it was Damon trying to get her attention.

Her attitude changed immediately. Her teeth gritted as she stepped back from him. "Get away from me."

He ignored her request. "Melanie, just hear me out." He could see that she was ignoring him, but he wanted to get his point across to her so he continued talking. "You never answer any of my calls or let me in the gallery when I come by, so I haven't been able to really apologize and better explain myself to you. I promise if you give me another chance, we can start clean and honest."

She cocked her head at him and said in a flat voice, "I was honest. You weren't. Goodbye." She walked off deeper into the crowd.

"Melanie. Melanie" Damon followed behind her trying to get close to her again. He saw that the crowd had thickened between them. He remembered the look of disgust she had in her eyes for him and the finality her 'goodbye' held, so he walked back to his corral with his head low cursing himself for the scheme he devised trying to get her. He knew he pushed away a good woman.

Melanie, still running through the crowd, looked back to see if she had finally lost Damon. When she turned her head back forward, she ran right into the back of a tall, muscular man. *Maybe this is my new beginning!* She laughed inwardly at herself as the man teetered forward trying not to lose his balance. Melanie threw her arms out quickly causing them to encase his body to try and keep him from falling at all.

He smelled good to her as she held on to him.

The man gently gripped her hands as he regained his balance. He turned around to face her with her arms still wrapped around him. He looked down at her and smiled. "Melanie."

"Aaron." Embarrassed, she blushed and pulled back from him.

He allowed her to put some distance between them, but he still held her hands.

"I didn't know if I would see you here today, but I was hoping I would. It's been too long, Mel." He stared in her eyes as he pulled her hand up to his lips and kissed the back of it. His eyes never left hers.

Melanie pulled her hands from his and created more distance between them. She fanned herself. She knew she wasn't only hot from the sun beaming down on her at that moment, but more so, from the look in Aaron's eyes and the gentle way he kissed her hand. *Dang, he still makes me giddy whenever he kisses my hand.*

She cleared her throat to speak up. *Maybe saying something now will divert his intense stare at me.* "Yeah. It's been a while. I've been busy and well, you know how things ended the last time we saw each other." She looked past him. She wished the race would start already so she wouldn't have to talk to him anymore. She had already been burying memories of him the past months, but him being in front of her played with her emotions in an unsettling way for her.

He drew closer to her. "Mel, I wish you would believe me. I didn't know Damon was using what I was telling him about you against me."

"And why were you telling him anything about me in the first place?" Melanie folded her arms at her chest waiting for Aaron to respond.

"Because woman, you were driving me insane resisting what was happening between us." Aaron tightened his lips as he laughed. "I needed someone to talk to, a sounding board to help me figure out how to win you over."

Melanie huffed. "Why do you want me?" Her face softened.

"Why do I want you? Why do I want you? Why wouldn't I want you? Have you met yourself?"

Melanie gave him a too-quick smile.

"You are an amazing woman. If I feel so strongly about you with the months we spent together, I can only imagine how deeply in love with you I would be if we hadn't separated."

"Separated? We were never a couple."

"There may not have been a title on it, but our hearts and spirits had an understanding. Am I lying?" He narrowed his eyes in on her.

Melanie poked her lips out and rocked back and forth on her heels trying to ignore him.

He laughed. "You can make that 'whatever' face all you want, but you know I'm telling the truth." He reached out and grabbed her hands into his as he stepped even closer to her. "Look around you. Does it look like people care that I'm holding your hands like this?" He held up their intertwined hands high for her to see.

Melanie scanned the crowd near her. Most were oblivious to her and Aaron. She caught the eye of a white woman that smiled at her. She continued to scam her surroundings to see a black man rubbing his white wife's shoulders. She even looked up to see a black woman give her a thumbs up before she turned her attention back to Aaron. "Yeah, well, that's just this crowd. What about all the other bad experiences we've had being out together?"

"So, what about them?" Aaron's voiced raised a pitch higher than his normal voice. "I'm certain the good experiences will outweigh the bad ones if we keep living." Aaron looked in her eyes and could tell she needed some more reassuring. "Look, Mel, I know you think us being together is complicated, but isn't life complicated?"

"Yeah, so why make it worse?" She tried to pull back from him, but he pulled her into him and wrapped his arms around her waist.

"I say as long as we're together everything will be alright."

"Well, what about you and Damon's friendship? I dated both of y'all, so won't that be odd if you and I gave it a go again but he's still around?"

"You don't have to worry about him. Clearly we weren't ever really friends, so ending that fakeship was necessary."

"I don't know, Aaron. I admit, I like you a lot—"

"You what?" Aaron smiled and turned his ear towards her mouth.

"I said I like you—"

"You what?" Aaron pulled her closer to him.

She looked up at him. "Yes, Aaron. I really do like you. I'll be honest enough to say I really do care about you."

"So then, let's do it."

"What?" Melanie raised one eyebrow.

"Let's make us exclusive. We can go as slow as you want us to, but let's just be together, grow together." Aaron's eyes pleaded with Melanie's.

She stood stiff in his arms. *What to do, Melanie? What to do, Lord? Can I trust myself? Should I trust myself?* She looked into Aaron's eyes and saw nothing but sincere admiration and care for her. A calm overtook her. "Okay." A smile slowly crept across her face. "I guess if life has to be complicated at times, then I might as well live it and enjoy it with the ones and those things that are worth the complications."

Aaron winked at her and leaned down to kiss her. He pecked at her lips before he covered her mouth with his.

"And, go! Good luck, runners," the announcer said, signaling the first corral of runners to proceed.

Melanie took off running full speed ahead. She looked back at Aaron. "Come on, keep up."

He smiled and quickly caught in stride beside her. He reached down and knitted his fingers with hers as he looked over at her. "Naw, we'll do this together."

Other Books Available

(Best if you read Forever Friends series before reading Sisterhood Chronicles 3)

ABOUT THE AUTHOR

Anita Davis is a former elementary teacher born and raised in Chicago. Although she wrote short stories much of her childhood, she didn't unlock and cultivate her passion as a writer until she became a writing teacher for middle school students. The more she had to create sample writings for her students, the more she realized her passion and ability to tell stories in the written form. She decided to hone her craft as a writer by completing her Master of Fine Arts in Creative Writing via National University. She now pursues writing books most of her time, in addition to being a flight attendant. Anita seeks to encourage, engage, and entertain her readers.

She is Co-Founder of Book Euphoria, a group of Chicago authors bound by their love of literature. Book Euphoria hosts literary events and they also founded the empowerment movement, Black Girl Passion.

Anita writes contemporary romantic women's fiction and seeks to encourage, engage, and entertain her readers.

authoranitadavis@gmail.com
www.authoranitadavis.com
Facebook: Anita Davis and Author page: Author Anita Davis
Instagram: @authoranitadavis   Twitter: @_AnitaDavis